With special thanks to

Tegan Baker

Mandy Ansell

Paul Ansell

Louise Ansell

Roisin Mcgovern

Mark Swarley

Astrotheon: Keepers of Concorvia

By J. A. Ansell

Chapter One: Bedtime Story

"Jariko!" called a loving voice that travelled through the house.

"Jariko!" she called again, but the sound of her voice fell flat in the silence of the house. She moved swiftly across the living room to the stairs leading to the second floor of the old wooden house.

The living room consisted of a stone fireplace with a wooden table not too far from it and two wooden chairs. Pots and pans lived in the opposite corner of the room under the stairs on an old wooden set of drawers, most of the cooking happened at the table but she liked to keep the pots clean and away from the fire in case they got covered in soot. Being one of two rooms in the house, the living room also had a bear skin bed roll and rolled up blanket used as a pillow. This is where she slept; it wasn't much but the fire kept her warm in the winter.

"You better not be hiding again," she called, this time with a firmness to her voice. As she began to climb the wooden staircase, she listened but all she could hear was the creak of the wood and the whistle of the wind filling the silence.

As she reached the top of the stairs, she stopped and called again, "Jariko, if you're going to try and scare me you will sleep outside with the horse."

She would never make her own child sleep outside in the cold; it was nothing more than an empty threat. She slowly made her way to the window, pulling open the curtains and looking out to the woods behind their house. Suddenly, a small boy dropped from the roof hanging off the ledge, screaming as he did so. He was no older than seven or eight with long blonde hair, and deep blue eyes. His cheshire grin was filled with shining white teeth and he had a scar down his left cheek. No one could remember how he got it but most likely due to his own curiosity or stupidity.

"Did I scare you mother?" He said with a smirk on his face as he climbed back into the house.

"One day you're going to be the death of me!" She shouted, holding her chest and stumbling for the stool at the top of the stairs. She stared at Jariko for a moment and tried to keep a stern look, but the look on her little boy's face was too much and she broke into laughter.

"I got you good," he said proudly while putting his hands on his waist, both of them laughing together.

"Yes, you did but it's dark, you need to go to bed." Jariko's smile quickly disappeared as he threw his hands down in a strop and started to walk to his room, the only other room in the house.

It was more of an attic, converted into a room when Jariko was born, so it was small. All it had was a wooden bedside table with a half-burned candle on top of it and another bed roll laid out next to it. Jariko kept his clothes in a pile in the corner of the room next to his mother's clothes that were neatly folded. Jariko liked to clean his own clothes, it made him feel like a grown-up but usually his mother would re-wash them when he was out playing in the woods.

Just as he reached the doorway he quickly turned and said, "Can you tell me a story before bed?" slapping his hands together begging for a story.

"Of course, what story would you like to hear?" She said while walking into Jariko's room.

"Tell me the story of the Creators again, please." It was his favourite story to listen to and he also knew it was a long story so he could stay up late.

"But I told you that one a few days ago, wouldn't you like to hear about the Gnomes of the North, or maybe tales of the Great Crusaders - oh, what about the Keepers? The brave knights who protect Concorvia?" She looked at him and she could tell from his face that he wasn't interested. "As stubborn as your father," she said smiling as she sat down on the bedroll. Jariko laid down and rested his head on his mother's lap raising his arm and grabbing her hand.

"I'm ready," he said letting out a short yawn, but forcing his mouth closed so it seemed like he wasn't tired. She put her other hand on his head and started to stroke his hair as she began the story.

"A very long time ago, there were seven beings that we call the Creators. These were creatures of great power that lived before the universe, before life and before you and me. They simply called this place the Void, an empty place, but at the same time full and endlessly expanding, but at the same time small. This was the place they were born and the place they have lived for longer than we can even understand.

However, these creatures had too much power and one day the power became unbearable to control and turned into a threat to their lives. The leader of the Creators, Primak spent countless hours or maybe even centuries trying to find a way to save himself and his brothers and sister, but he just could not find a way to keep the power and survive. Until Tando, the last-born Creator, approached him and presented a solution. He told Primak that if they all released their power into the empty space in which they lived then while their power recharged it would buy them time to figure out a more permanent solution. Primak was hesitant but agreed as it was the only idea they had."

Jariko sprung up onto his knees making a loud thud as he did so, "But he was lying wasn't he mother?" he exclaimed loudly.

Jariko's mother was not impressed, putting her hands on her hips and with a stern voice said, "How about we finish the story and find out?"

Jariko slouched his head as he laid back down.

"As I was saying, Primak knew it was the only chance they had. The seven Creators gathered, linked hands and began to focus their power into the centre of the circle. A glowing orb began to take shape. Constantly changing and swirling like waves of the ocean, changing from a purple to blue to green, endlessly shifting. This was a ball of pure magic, the more it grew the hotter it became and you could feel the power pulsing from within, but suddenly Tando let go of his fellow Creators' hands causing the orb of power to become unstable. Primak screamed as he reached out a hand to grab Tando but at that moment his concentration swayed, and the orb exploded with such power that it tore the very space around them, creating our universe."

Jariko sat up once again and he looked at his mother, "That was called the big bang, right?" he asked, trying to remember from the last time he heard the story.

"Yes, that's right, but there is still a lot more of the story to go and we will never make it to the end if you keep interrupting me."

Jariko said nothing, he just laid back down on the bed roll.

"After the explosion, the Creators were near death, if they could even die. They floated there in the new universe. Primak was still conscious, trying to compose himself but all he could focus on was the unbearable cold. He had never experienced a feeling like this before and it wasn't pleasant. After minutes that felt like years, Tando appeared in front of him. He didn't seem damaged by the explosion but seemed to be trying to adjust to the new sensations like Primak was. Tando stopped for a moment and just as Primak was falling into unconsciousness he saw Tando lift his right hand and in one quick motion severe his left hand. He flinched but didn't show any sign of major pain as a new hand materialised in its place, he then focused on the severed hand and closed his eyes, muttered a few words and the arm began to glow. He was sealing his power into his severed hand using it as a vessel for his power. Just like before, an orb began to form enveloping the severed hand and growing in shape. Tando did this so he could still use all his power by drawing it from his vessel but once he had finished imbuing his power into this orb he too drifted into a deep sleep. Over time the seven Creators floating in space emitted cocoon-like auras that surrounded their bodies and protected them, helping them stay alive. But objects floating in space began to clash with them and stick to these cocoons, growing and forming stone coffins for each of the Creators. However, while this was happening Tando's magic kept swelling and heating, melting anything that came close into pure molten rock. Unlike the other six Creators Tando's aura grew tenfold until it was so heavy and dense that nearby objects began to orbit it including the six cocoons of the other Creators. Over millions of years this became known as our solar system, with each of the six Creators becoming the planets and Tando's magic being our sun."

Jariko raised his hand and waited there for a few seconds. Jariko's mother smiled as she said, "Yes, Jariko?"

“If the six Creators became planets, which one do we live on?” he replied, lowering his hand back down onto his stomach.

“You always do pick up on things quickly, don't you?” She said smiling while running her fingers through Jariko’s hair. “We live on the most powerful of them all; our home is Primak.” Jariko smiled but without realising released a big yawn, obviously tired from being up so late. “I guess this is as good a place to stop as any,” she said while standing up to blow out the candle.

“No please, I'm not even tired yet!” Jariko explained desperately, “We are just getting to the good bit!” Jariko’s mother stood there for a second, silently trying to decide.

“I'll clean the stable out all by myself in the morning, I swear.”

She didn't usually give in to the bribes, but she did hate cleaning out the horse.

“Fine, but no playing adventure til it's done.”

Jariko nodded. She sat back down and Jariko’s face lit up with excitement as he crossed his legs and stared at her ready for his favourite part of the story.

“Okay where was I... ah yes, the war of creation. No one knows how long the creators were floating in space before they awoke, but I would bet it was longer than any of us can imagine. The first to wake up was Tando - having all his power still at his disposal he was able to recover a little quicker. He embraced the cold soundless void, and he found himself trying to take in as much of it in as he could. It had changed a lot since he had last laid eyes upon it. He could sense the presence of the other Creators, but he couldn't see them. After a few moments of confusion, he realised there were six planetoids orbiting him, slowly and far away. All of the Creators have almost a sixth sense to see where the others are and from their energy alone, they can tell each other apart. Quarbela was the closest and Termatil next to her. Primak was in front of him a little further away and Quintala and Sacula a little further on. Saxunda was by himself on the left, the furthest away. Tando was angry they were still alive, but he was not surprised; he knew there was nothing they could do to him now but curious he travelled to one of the planets to gloat over his victory. He travelled to Primak, but when he arrived, he was shocked at what he found.

There was life on the planet. Small creatures and plants that had come about from nothing. Tando was speechless; the Creators had never seen conscious life other than themselves. He carried on exploring the planet seeing all it had created while he slumbered. Mountains, rivers and a great sea covered the planet's surface and all kinds of creatures of all shapes and sizes populated every inch of the planet. Tando was speechless and amazed by what he had found until it all culminated into pure rage at the thought that Primak had still been able to do something like this even after Tando had beaten him. Obviously Primak had no part in this but millennia of jealousy focused Tando’s rage at Primak, rage so strong Tando did something he didn't plan to do. He awoke the other Creators.

Due to their massive loss of power, Tando had to give each Creator a little piece of his power and summoned them to the planet Primak. They were only apparitions of each Creator, a projection of their consciousness. They all appeared in front of him one by one. Quarbela was first, then Termatil and Quintala, then Sacula followed shortly by Saxunda and Primak was last.

Obviously, each of the Creators was furious about Tando's betrayal but were unable to do anything to him. After what we can only imagine was a heated discussion, Primak asked why he had awoken them. After seeing how Primak's planet had thrived he explained he wanted to host a competition and the winner would be given a piece of Tando's power to do with as they wished. Tando only did this because he knew that with his power, he could beat them at anything and prove that he's better once and for all. They all agreed and Tando told them the competition. Inspired by all this new life, they would see who could create the deadliest creature. They would have seven days and they all could create whatever they wanted..." She was about to continue the story but then she noticed Jariko was fast asleep.

She didn't know how long he had been asleep for, but she was probably talking to herself for a while. She smiled while letting out a soft chuckle. She lifted his head slowly off her lap and gently placed it on the rolled-up blanket, which was his pillow, gave him a kiss on his forehead, grabbed the candle and walked over to the door. She looked back at her son and stared at him for a few moments then her soft grin lowered, and her face turned sad, a tear ran down her rosy cheek, dripping onto the floor. It was a face you would only ever see on a concerned and loving mother. She wiped her face with her sleeve and her soft grin crept back.

"Good night, my love," she whispered as she closed the door.

Chapter Two: Alone at Home

The warm rays of the sun leaked through the cracks in between the curtains of Jariko's window. Jariko was already awake and looking up at the ceiling, he watched the dusty air dance through the rays of sunlight in his room. Because his window was east facing, he would wake up at the crack of dawn but liked to lay down and think. He wouldn't usually get up until the light was blinding in his eyes. When he was a child, he would jump out of bed and go see his mother the second he woke up but ever since she died six years ago, he struggled to wake up as easily.

He hated waking up to an empty house, he hated being alone, but he and his mother had lived in this old cabin since he was a child, far away from anyone who he could have a conversation with. The closest town was Rybalin, a small trading town on the west coast of Concorvia, the country he lived in. Rybalin was half a day's walk away, so he only went there when he needed his medicine, which happened to be today. When he remembered this, it motivated him to get out of bed and get dressed.

Being the only time he saw other people, his trips to Rybalin were the only things he looked forward to. All other days he spent tending to his mother's small garden which had a variety of vegetables: carrots, cabbage, peas, broccoli, an apple tree a small walk from his house and mushrooms tended to grow in the area. He mostly ate vegetables and fruit because he wasn't much of a hunter; he tried to kill a chicken he found wandering in the woods once but when he went to grab it a dozen more came out from what seemed like thin air and chased him away. He hadn't tried to catch anything since.

Truth be told, Jariko knew he wouldn't have been able to harm the chicken, he was just desperate at the time. He was trying to grow his first crops, but it wasn't going too well. That was a hard year, that was the first summer after his mother had gone. Occasionally he went fishing and caught fish but he wasn't good at that either so that was only on the rarest of occasions. His mother taught him how to cook bread and a handful of other pastries, but ingredients were expensive, so he only did this on his birthday.

They did keep animals on their small farm but Jariko had grown so fond of the animals as a child that he didn't have the heart to kill them. He had been like that ever since he was a young boy and once he made friends with the pig, he named it Snort. His mother would try and convince him they needed the meat, but he was adamant that if she harmed Snort he would run away. It was an empty threat but his mother saw the look in his eyes and gave in.

After that, they became vegetarians willingly or not, but it did help them save their gold. It was around this time that Jariko's mother bought their horse and Jariko named him Runner. This was an ironic name, however, because the only thing Runner didn't do was run.

"Slowest horse in the land," the man said when they bought Runner, but Jariko felt sorry for him so they took him home and his mother taught him how to ride. Runner was Jariko's best friend; they would go for slow walks around the woods and pretend they were on a great adventure in distant lands. Of course, in reality Jariko would sit on Runner's back as he grazed the fields, hardly moving at all, but Jariko didn't care.

For as long as he could remember he wanted to go on a grand adventure filled with danger and excitement and gold, lots of gold, but there were no adventures in these lands. The only people who travelled the lands were the Keepers, the knights sworn to protect the king and Concorvia, but the only people who could get knighted were the most skilled warriors or the most powerful mages and Jariko was neither so he only had the long boring walks from his house to Rybalin and back again and nothing ever happened on these walks.

Jariko knew that today was going to be the same as every other trip to town but he prepared himself anyway, grabbing his pack and filling it with some water and a few apples for the journey. He couldn't get much in his pack, it was small and only had one strap that he had to sling over his head. He couldn't afford a new one but this one did the job.

Once he knew he had everything he might need, he grabbed the most important thing, his poncho. It was an old family heirloom that his mother told him had been in the family for generations. It was a large poncho covering most of his body with a faded purple colour which had mostly worn to a dull grey now. You could tell how old it was from the large amount of repair work done to it but because of this the original pattern and decoration was almost completely gone, apart from a few swirls and lines scattered throughout the material. Jariko used to hate having such an ugly piece of clothing, it reminded him how poor he and his mother were, but it was the last gift she ever gave him just before she died. When she gave it to him, she made him swear that no matter what happened if he left the farm or saw any people, he needed to wear it. She said it would protect him. His mother was always very protective, never letting Jariko go to town without her or even leave the farm alone but when she died it must have given her peace of mind knowing he had the poncho, so Jariko agreed and gave his word to always wear it. Even though Jariko hated wearing it, after so long it had become his most prized possession, almost feeling as if his mother was still hugging him when he wore it so he kept his word, only taking it off to wash it or himself.

He was now ready to set off for Rybalin, he walked outside and put a rope around Runner's neck and set off.

There wasn't a lot to see on the walk. Jariko's cabin sat at the base of a large mountain north of Rybalin. There were a few acres of woods then open fields and hills and a thin dirt road. You could just about see a few houses dotting the horizon as you walked along the road but nothing special. Occasionally you would meet some other travellers walking and they would nod and Jariko would nod back but there were never any words spoken. The road was a bit too inland to get close to the sea but Jariko could smell the salt of the ocean and feel the cool sea breeze on his face.

When he was a child on the rarest occasions his mother would take him to the seaside to watch the waves, Jariko always wanted to be a sailor and travel the oceans and see other lands but he could never leave his mother back then. Now it was more fear that kept him home. Fear that if he left, he would never come back and lose the few memories of his mother he had left. Now he never went to the seaside even though he could go every day if he wanted to but he tried to stay away to make it easier on himself - out of sight, out of mind, he thought. He marched on down the dirt road.

Three hours or so had passed before he could see Rybalin in the distance, as always not a lot happened but he did meet a friendly dog who was quickly called away by his master. That made Jariko smile, he always wanted a dog, but dogs were very expensive, more expensive than horses. Runner basically fed himself but if Jariko couldn't even have meat himself how could he get some for a dog? It was just a dream for now.

Jariko had finally arrived - it was a large town on the west coast of Concorvia, all the buildings were single floor wooden cabins with straw rooftops and a single door and window, the whole city had a single dirt road connecting every house around the each of town. This was called Beggars Row due to the large amount of homeless people that came to Rybalin to work but were turned away due to their poor health, smell, or any reason the sailors and shopkeepers could think of. Because of this the only place they could sleep and stay dry was in between each cabin, clinging to the walls. Some even dug little trenches on the side of the houses to crawl in like rats.

At the centre of the city was a large open piece of land where the town hall used to stand before it was burned down because of the rise in taxes many years ago. The town never had the money or the interest in rebuilding it, so the villagers set up a market to fill the space, however thanks to this the city had developed a reputation and fame for the market and people travelled from all over to buy and sell.

It was one of Concorvia's largest trading ports sitting at the edge of a large lake of water that was connected to the sea by a narrow gap in the mountain side. Thanks to this it was easy to control the ships coming into the port, however by land it was easier for bandits to attack the town, because of this a large ten-foot wooden wall surrounding the town was erected with a large gate at the front. The docks were always full of ships and boats from a country down south called Dawn's Delivery, but they called it Domadon. It was a strange country, but it was the home to the Empire of the Marvub. One of the beast races, the monkey people, (but don't let them hear you call them monkeys), they are small but extremely fast and dangerous plus their country has a lot of materials and produce unavailable in Concorvia so they trade it here in Rybalin and then it travels down south to the capital Orkestra, but the food is always freshest when it arrives here.

Jariko tied Runner to a wooden post outside the town.

"Stay here, you hear me, don't eat your rope and wander off again. I need you to carry my supplies home."

Runner looked at him and let out a squeaky fart.

"I'll take that as a yes," Jariko said turning round and heading for the gate.

The town itself wasn't too busy - the sailors tended to stay on their ships, they didn't like carrying the cargo any further than they needed to, so the town was mostly filled with people collecting supplies from the market although these crowds of people were diverse enough as it was.

Humans were the biggest part of the population, but they lived with the race of Gormen also known as Goblins. They aren't too different to humans, but they have milky green skin and long pointy ears drooping down the side of their heads. There are also the Elchrit also known as Elves, or specifically the Forgotten Elves, who have sickly yellow skin with pointy ears as well but theirs stick up towards the sky. They are mostly traders that will con you out of your last gold coin.

Jariko's mother told him never to buy something from them because you always lose. These Elchrit and Gormen are the most civilised of their races. Of course, you also have Pact Goblins and Blood-Elves, barbarians who live in the woods to the east and even the Roach-lins. Jariko's mother used to tell him scary stories of how they came out of the ground and stole bad children, obviously made up but it still scared young Jariko into behaving. Goblins and Forgotten Elves have lived with humans for a very long time and these three races make up most of the populations in every town in Concorvia. Some towns have small families of beast races and you see travellers every other week but the most common beast race is the Tunere, these are turtle-like people who are the most skilled blacksmiths on Primak. Able to make the deadliest weapons out of steel or even their shells when they outgrow them and drop off. Tunere shells are one of the strongest materials on the market but very expensive because it takes a long time for their shells to fall off, although when you live for two hundred years you probably don't notice the time it takes. All these races lived together relatively happily and in Rybalin it was common to see such diverse crowds of different species, so when Jariko walked through the gates he paid no attention and continued on with his day.

It had been raining the night before so every step Jariko took made a squelch as he walked down the road deeper into the city, jumping over all the puddles and dodging the crowds of people, as he broke into a slow jog. If you didn't stick to the roads it was very easy to get lost but because Rybalin was a large circle it wasn't too hard to find your way back eventually, you just needed to keep following the road until you found yourself back at the gate and then you could just try again.

However, Jariko had basically grown up in this town so he knew every shortcut, dodging all the beggars and stray animals also being careful not to touch the walls of each cabin because when they weren't muddy and rotten, they were covered from top to bottom in splinters and broken shards of wood. Other than that, it was a nice run through the city as he made his way to the stretch of shops on the east side of the city. Every shop had a wooden sign hanging above the door: Dandoor's Steel Arms, Mages Assortents, Judelen's Tools, Wooden Splinter and Rolo's Bubbles - this was where Jariko was heading.

It was run by a sweet old Goblin called Rolo, but Jariko called him old man Rolo. He had needed his medicine since he was a child, so Rolo was a close family friend, however this didn't stop Jariko getting nervous. He was starting to need more medicine than normal, and he didn't have the gold to pay for more. If he didn't get his medicine, it would be a big problem because he wouldn't be able to tend to his crops and they would die, he would run out of food and then he too would die. So, it was crucial he got more of his medicine, but Jariko had no money and didn't know how to convince Rolo to give it to him for free. Jariko opened the door and standing a few feet in front of him behind a counter covered with bottles and odd plants and ingredients was old man Rolo. He was a short Goblin only about five feet in height and a glistening bald head besides a few curly hairs on the top. His skin was wrinkled from a long life of smiling and as green as some of his potions, a handful of teeth and long brown robes down to the floor that looked like his bed sheets held on by a rope around his waist.

"Well, hello young Jariko," he said in a shrill voice, "Have you run out already, or are you here to see me?" The old goblin said chuckling to himself. Jariko smiled.

"Both," Jariko said.

"Maybe I need to increase the dosage so you get more out of a bottle," Rolo said as he stumbled around under the counter looking for Jariko's parcel.

"I think that would be good, I noticed it's starting to wear off quicker now," Jariko said worried that he would not have enough gold in his pocket. Rolo stood up with a parcel in his hand and placed it on the counter.

"Well, you have grown a lot in the last few years and I will need to adjust it accordingly. And don't worry, this one's on the house."

Jariko looked shocked, "How did y.."

"I can see it in your eyes, young Jariko," the old goblin said laughing. "I promised your mother I would look after you and this is the least I can do."

Jariko smiled, he tried to hide it, but he was too relieved.

"Thanks, old man, I owe you one," he exclaimed, as he left the shop waving.

Rolo waved back as he shouted, "You stay safe, young man!" laughing as he waved back.

As he was walking away from the shop Jariko's smile turned serious and determined.

"I really need to start making serious money," Jariko said to himself, "I can't leach off of old man Rolo forever."

Chapter Three: Unexpected Visitors

After collecting his medicine Jariko went to the market to spend some of his gold on essentials he needed.

As he was looking through the market, he overheard two men chatting, "Did you hear? The guards turned away a group of merchants this morning?" The first man said.

"Apparently they had enough weapons and armour to fight an ogre!" He said in disbelief while drinking from a tankard filled with ale.

"Wonder what they were doing in these parts."

"I dunno," the second man replied, "But whatever they were doing they weren't selling vegetables. Maybe they were looking for that witch!"

The first man quivered in his boots at the thought, then leant in to try and whisper.

“I heard she can make a man do anything, all she has to do is say the words,” he said, leaning in further. “Even murder.” They both looked extremely unsettled. Jariko knew exactly who they were talking about; her wanted poster was up in every shop in town.

WANTED, Sireana Silvertongue. Extremely dangerous sorceress. Do not approach. Dead or Alive 10,000 gold.

Jariko had daydreamed of finding and catching her, but what could he do against a sorceress?

“Mother used to say that I was unusually strong, but what's strength gonna do to a magic user? If the stories are true she will just tell me to kill myself and I’m done,” Jariko said to himself, shaking his head. “Would be nice to have that money though and Jariko the bounty hunter sounds pretty good,” he continued daydreaming while he shopped.

He picked up a small bag of salt, a box of nails, some thread and a beetroot for Runner. Jariko didn't know why, but for some reason Runner would do anything for beetroot. Hang a piece of beetroot off of some string and a stick and that's the closest Runner would get to being a trained horse.

Jariko left town and went to the post where he left Runner. By some miracle he was still there laying on his side on the ground. Runner always did this after a walk and people usually thought he was dead. It discouraged people from stealing him so Jariko didn't mind, although he did get some strange looks while he was trying to pick Runner up.

He finally got Runner to his feet using some of the beetroot he had bought, and they headed home. Along the way Jariko witnessed something strange - while trotting along the dirt track about halfway home he saw two men standing in the distance in the corner of his eye. He would often pass people on his way to and from town, but this was different. These two men were hunched over with cloaks covering half of their bodies but from what he could see their bodies were disproportionate, with thin legs and standing on the balls of their feet like a cat and arms curled into their chest. Whatever they were they weren't humans, Goblins or Elves or at least not like any Jariko had ever seen up until that point. Runner must have spotted them too because suddenly he was jumping and bucking around. Jariko pulled on his reins to calm him down but then suddenly as quickly as he noticed them, they were gone. He looked around trying to see where they were but the only thing, he could see was a bird flying high in the sky. He stood there for a second a little uneasy but realised that the sun was going down and pushed the thought out of his mind. He was probably just tired and imagined it, he took a quick sip of his bottle of fresh medicine and hurried home.

They got home a little quicker than normal, the strange encounter had even spooked Runner enough to travel a little faster, but when they arrived home, something was wrong. His door was open. Already being as freaked out as he was, Jariko walked Runner to his stable and closed the door while grabbing the wooden axe that was leant on the outside of the stable.

"The door could've just blown open from the wind," he whispered to himself, but he knew this wasn't true. Ever since his mother died, he triple-checked everything he did to make sure it was done right and when he left each day he tied the door shut with some rope. He knew that he tied it that morning before he left and as he slowly got closer, he couldn't see the rope. Whoever opened the door took it inside with them. There wasn't anything to steal in the house, but the story of the sorceress had him on edge.

What if she's inside, what if she makes me her slave or worse? Jariko thought to himself. He wanted to run away but his legs kept slowly moving to the door; the thought of leaving his mother's house to a criminal witch didn't sit right with him. Suddenly he was at the front door standing perfectly still, waiting to see if he could hear something. Then footsteps and voices echoed softly through the house, his heart started to race faster and faster.

"*Those are women's voices,*" he thought, "*Could it be Sireana*?"

His legs began to shake.

I'll go in quick and kill her before she can speak a word. I can do this... but it sounds like there's two of them, which one is she? What does she look like? If I kill the wrong one, I'm dead.

The task seemed increasingly impossible the more he thought about it. Suddenly a wave of courage swept over him, he took a deep breath and just charged into the house regardless of the danger. He charged for the two women, he lifted his axe above his head and then swung with all his might.

It took Jariko a second to realise that the axe wasn't in his hands anymore. He slowly looked up above his head and there was the axe, floating in the air above him.

“What are you doing?” A soft, slightly insulted voice asked.

Jariko looked straight ahead and in front of him were two beautiful women dressed in short white robes folded over and tied with a belt. The older one was a goblin standing in the kitchen area with a knife in her hand but not in a threatening way - she was cutting vegetables. She had clear pale green skin, black hair, and yellow eyes. Jariko got the idea that this woman was wealthy judging by the jewelled necklace that hung around her neck. She must have been about the same age as Jariko’s mother and she was just as beautiful as she was.

He then looked over at the other younger human woman, no older than Jariko. She had dark chestnut hair, white skin and blue eyes that looked almost glowing in the sunlight. Jariko was more than a little mesmerised by her and this made it harder for him to concentrate on the situation. He was so struck by her face that he barely noticed her arm stretch out towards him. It took a few seconds for Jariko to understand the situation.

"Are you a sorceress?" He asked, choking on fear.

"Duh," she said, rolling her eyes at the stupidity of the question, "And who are you?"

Jariko paused before he answered. He didn't want to tell them his name, but he had to give a good enough answer, so they didn't kill him.

"This is my house!" He said standing up straight trying to regain some dignity. The axe fell from above Jariko's head and lodged into the floor inches from his feet. This scared Jariko again, instantly losing the last of his dignity as he flinched.

"Liar" the young girl said, "Where would a kid like you get the money for a house like this?" Jariko wasn't used to telling anyone about his life or his mother, but he saw no other way to diffuse the situation.

"It was my mother's house, she died six years ago and left it to me."

It was hard for him to talk about his mother.

"Six years?" the older woman put down the knife and walked over to Jariko, "You've been alone for six years? You poor thing."

There was something about her voice that reminded Jariko of his mother, which calmed him down.

"I'm sorry for my apprentice, she can be a little hot headed, and I'm sorry for entering your house without your permission. We saw the empty stable and run-down cabin and assumed it was abandoned."

Jariko found this easy to believe as without his mother cleaning every day the cabin was in terrible condition.

"We have been traveling for a long time so when we saw a dry house and food we couldn't help ourselves. How about we finish making dinner and we can share our stories?" She smiled as she said this and even her smile reminded Jariko of his mother, so he agreed, not saying a word just giving a nod and walking over to the table and sat down.

At this point in time Jariko didn't know what to do, say or even think. Two complete strangers were cooking him dinner. It seemed so surreal but at the same time he had been so lonely for so long it felt almost comforting to have them there. It had been six years since anyone besides Jariko had stepped a foot inside this house, besides Runner when he just turned up some mornings. He didn't know if he could trust them, he didn't even know their names but the amazing smell coming from the pot on the fire was too distracting to think clearly. It was a sweet smell that seemed to warm Jariko's soul. The older goblin grabbed three bowls while the younger girl carried the pot to the table - she was using magic again. Carefully suspending the pot in mid-air, you could see in her face she was concentrating to keep the pot upright. Jariko's mother told him about magic and some of the things sorcerers could do but he had never seen it in person. He didn't have time to be amazed however, he had to figure out if they were a threat. What if one of them really was Sireana? Then he came up with a plan, he needed them to tell him to do something and see if he could resist.

"Hope you're hungry?" The Goblin woman said, "It's a special recipe." She smiled at Jariko trying to figure out if he had calmed down. She poured him a bowl of stew.

"I don't have a spoon," Jariko said.

"Go grab your own spoon," snapped the apprentice. Jariko didn't move; he refused, awkwardly sitting there in silence but he was now sure that the young apprentice wasn't Sireana, which made him feel better.

"Don't be so rude Irabella, it's not like we were invited, it's the least you could do." The apprentice looked at her almost as if she was about to throw a tantrum like Jariko used to when his mother made him take a bath.

"So, what's your name young man?" He didn't see any reason not to tell them his name.

"It's Jariko."

"Well, nice to meet you Jariko, my name's Mutana and that's Irabella." She held out her hand and Jariko shook it.

"And you really live out here all by yourself?" Jariko didn't want to answer too many questions until he was sure she wasn't a criminal, then he had an idea. The apprentice walked over and handed him a spoon and he began to eat. At the same time he began to tap his foot on the floor, faster and faster.

“Jariko? Did you hear me?” Mutana asked. Jariko continued to tap his foot.

“Hello? Answer her,” Irabella demanded. He could tell this was annoying them, he did it as a child to annoy his mother when he felt mischievous. He continued to tap faster.

“Jariko please, we aren't here to hurt you. Just talk to us.” He kept tapping, tap tap tap.

“Jariko stop tapping your foot and talk to us!” Mutana shouted. He didn't stop until Irabella stood up and grabbed Jariko by the collar of his poncho. There was no way to be sure and it wasn't a good plan, but they had both told him to do something and he didn't do it. He had no reason to believe they wouldn't have used magic on him if they could. It wasn't much but it was enough to convince Jariko neither were the criminal witch.

“I’m sorry, I'm just not used to having guests. Yes, all by myself for six years.” The two women looked confused at each other but now Jariko could relax.

“My mother died when I was ten,” Jariko explained.

“I'm sorry to hear that,” Mutana said, trying to forget the last few minutes. Irabella stayed quiet while eating on the other side of the table.

“That does mean you two are almost the same age,” Mutana said giggling and winked at Irabella.

“Don't be gross, I'm an entire year older than him,” Irabella said. This comment seemed to really annoy her but Jariko did notice her blush.

“Well, since you have opened up so much and you are obviously still uncomfortable, I'll tell you how we ended up here and where we are heading,” Mutana said as she finished her bowl of stew. “We are heading to Orkestra.”

Jariko stopped eating and his ears pricked up. Ever since he was a child he wanted to see Orkestra, the largest city in the world and capital of Concorvia. Jariko had always wanted to see the castle where the King of Concorvia sits and maybe someday meet the king himself.

“What are you doing in Orkestra?” Jariko asked, trying to pretend not to be interested.

“It's time to host the search for the new Grandmaster of the church. Whenever the current Grandmaster can’t run the church anymore they host a competition with the most powerful mages from each church around Concorvia to compete to see who will become the new leader.”

“Does that mean…” Jariko was interrupted by Irabella.

“Mutana is the most powerful sorceress from Ferradon, and I'm her best pupil.”

Chapter Four: A Lesson in Magic

Magic, much like any trade, takes years of training to master. There are five classes of magic, all harder than the last and every class has its levels of skill at which it can be used.

Class one: Perception magic, the teaching of controlling your own and others' senses. This is usually the magic used by mages who prefer sneaking to fighting. In its basic form one can turn invisible or improve their hearing to find prey miles away, but in the hands of a master they can cause you to see things that aren't really there. You think you're fighting the enemy but really you're trying to kill your companion. Due to its simplicity in casting it is the lowest form of magic.

Class two: Manipulation magic, the teaching of using your magic to manipulate objects also known as telekinesis. This is usually used for simple tasks and helping mages carry books or multitask, however pour enough magic into the spell and you can lift a city, or even fly. Due to Manipulation magic being so versatile and useful, it is usually the first kind of magic that mages are taught, although some are better than others.

Class three: Creation magic, the teaching of creating a Patrogorn, also known as Golems, which is a mindless sentinel made out of a material you touch when casting the spell. These can be made from stone to ice or even steel. Depending on the user of the spell this form of magic can turn the tide of any battle. While forming a nine foot stone Golem to fight for you is useful, in the hands of a master, a class three mage can create a Golem fifty feet tall around their own body to give them full control of the Golem and protect them from harm. This is why Creation magic is said to be the greatest defence.

Class four: Time magic, the teachings of slowing time. This class of magic has the least information about the topic and because of this it is the hardest to master but it can be a dangerous weapon. A person only has to relive a fight a dozen times and they will know what you're going to do before you do. However, the only known users are the Tunere monks who isolate themselves in the north, hidden within the mountains. Because of this there isn't much danger in finding a mage who can use Time magic but if an untrained mage unlocks time magic it can turn them insane if not used properly, eating away at their mind every time they use it.

Class five: Fabrication magic, the strongest form of magic, the teaching of forming your magic out of your body and turning it into anything you can imagine. The reason this is the most powerful of all the magic classes is because a class two mage can throw existing fire at a person but one who has mastery of Fabrication magic has the power to create fire from thin air. The only limit is the caster's imagination and depending on the size of their magic stores or magic pool, a class five mage can flood the area in water or make a sword of pure magic, but in battle it is a constant drain on the caster's energy so must be used sparingly depending on the caster.

There is also basic magic, there are not many uses for it especially in battle, but it is used more for party tricks and to gauge a mage's skill level when starting their training. Most commoners can learn basic magic down the tavern on a late night of drinking, but it is never more than a talking point and even this simplistic magic has been known to drain a person's magic so much they can collapse from exhaustion.

Every mortal on Primak has magic; it is there for anyone who is willing to learn how to use it. Magic comes from the Creators; however, no one can agree on the source of magic. Some say we get it from the sun – Tando's awesome power bleeds onto the planet as sunlight and gives it life. Others say it is Primak himself, down below powering life from inside the planet. It is impossible to know for sure, but we do know some are born to be a mage more so than others. This is what each school of magic looks for in pupils. They want children naturally born with a large pool of magic or just naturally gifted at using a certain class. In some rare cases a mage can use all classes of magic, but this hasn't been seen since the first mage – Agorith himself - who discovered magic and founded the church of Primak. He was the most powerful mage to ever be born and some say he never died. He had a great battle centuries ago, but his body was never recovered.

These stories made Jariko try to tap into his magic once before, but he couldn't even produce sparks from his fingers after hours of trying. At the time this deeply depressed Jariko but he soon found other ways of fighting and spending his time. The sadness dissipated to a simmering jealousy that he had learnt to accept.

If you wanted to learn more about how to use magic in Concorvia the church of Primak was where you went to learn. Since all magic comes from the Creators, every priest in the land who learnt about the gods would also unlock magic. For a good understanding of both, you would first learn about the science of how the universe works. All three things come hand in hand and when all three teachings are brought together a mage could unlock the ability to harness magic.

However, you could learn magic from outside sources but you would never get as powerful as the priests, and if anyone found out, you would be labelled a heathen; how can you truly appreciate magic and not thank the Creators who gifted it to you?

The church of Primak doesn't just focus on Primak's teachings but also the teachings of Quarbela and Quintala and teaches mostly class two, class three and class five magic respectively. However, this is just the way of Concorvia's church and religion. There are also two other main religions that are present in modern society.

There are also the temples in Deuterra to the north. They are looked after by the Turtle race called the Tunere. These monks do not believe in shedding their shells, thinking it brings them closer to the Creators, but their shells never stop growing and when they become too heavy to carry them, they sit at the top of a mountain and wait to die and meet their gods. Jariko always found this hard to believe when his mother told him - how would they get to the top of the mountain if they couldn't walk anymore? Probably just another story watered down over the years, changing and becoming more and more ridiculous.

In the Tunere temples they teach the ways of Sacula and time magic. They are not the most powerful mages, but they use magic more for meditation and teaching of patience more than battle like humans.

Finally, you have the temples to the south in Domadon. Not much is known about the monkey race called the Marvub and less is known about their religion. This is because most people never see the Marvub to ask them. They pay outside sources to deliver anything they trade with other countries and never get involved in diplomatic affairs; however, their Emperor is still regarded as one of the Five Titans of Primak. But if the stories are true, they follow Sacula, Termatil and Quarbela and teach Perception and Manipulation magic. Most people say they only teach these classes for stealing and tricking people. Jariko found this easy to believe - someone invisible with Manipulation magic could steal anything, especially if the Marvub are as nimble as the stories say.

As you can imagine with any belief system, each of these three groups believe that their way is the right way and any others are sacrilegious. They all believe their respective creators won the war of creation millennia ago. No one knows the true outcome, but they all have their different versions, but each version starts and ends the same way so Jariko could never understand the hatred each felt for one another. At the end of the day all three teach you how to be a better person and help you understand your place in this world, but no matter how silly it seemed to Jariko there have been countless wars over the centuries.

His mother taught him all about the wars and Jariko gained an almost unhealthy obsession with history and stories. He tried to memorise the date each war started and ended, how many people fought it and what each side got out of the bloodshed. Usually, they got nothing at all, but sometimes some good came out of the wars but it still never seemed worth it.

To lose so much life and loved ones over stories that could just be all made up didn't sit right with Jariko. He promised himself if he ever had the power to do so, he would stop all wars and bring peace. He knew it was silly but that was his dream, to create a world without war or at the very least help the world become more accepting of one another. He had no idea how he would ever accomplish this, but his mother always said he was destined for great things. Although that was a mother's job to encourage their children, so it didn't give Jariko much hope, but it was still nice to hear.

Chapter Five: New Friends

After dinner, the three sat around the fire as the sun began to set. Jariko had started to become more comfortable with the two sorceresses. He wanted to learn more about them and was fascinated by the stories they told him of their hometown and years of training with the mages in Ferradon. They spoke for hours about the city and their lives there, however Mutana had only lived there for a few years. She never said where she was actually from but Jariko got the idea she wasn't even from Concorvia. He wanted to ask where she was born but he didn't feel it was necessary to the conversation and didn't want to be rude and upset her. Jariko was interested in learning more about Irabella anyway. He was developing a bit of a crush on her, but this wasn't surprising - the only woman he had ever really spoken to was his mother and old man Rolo's wife.

It took a while for Irabella to open up and talk but after some persuading from Mutana and a few glasses of wine that they had brought with them, she began to tell the story of her childhood. She was orphaned and lived on the street for a long time, having to defend herself from men with ill intensions and Smoonum addicts, a drug favoured by the unlucky ones in society. It explained why she was so cold and scary but Jariko couldn't help but feel sorry for her. He had lived by himself for many years too, but he at least had the house and Rolo to look after him, she had no one.

As the day turned to night Jariko grew gradually more tired until Mutana asked.

"Would it be okay for us to stay here with you tonight Jariko? I fear it's too late in the day to head to Rybalin now."

Jariko nodded trying to hide his desperation to make them stay.

"My bed is upstairs, feel free to sleep there tonight, although it might be a little small for both of you," Jariko said, looking through a nearby crate for spare blankets.

“You’re too kind Jariko, your mother raised you well,” Mutana said smiling as Jariko handed her a blanket. “Irabella, why don't you stay down here with Jariko? I’m sure it will be warmer by the fire.”

Irabella didn't look happy at the idea but accepted it none the less and took another blanket from Jariko.

“Fine, but if I feel you're trying to cuddle me or anything else in the night I'll cut your nose off and feed it to your horse.”

This terrified Jariko - of course he wouldn't have done anything, but a threat like that made him think about sleeping outside with Runner just in case.

“Of course not!” Jariko exclaimed, his voice breaking from fear. He moved the chairs and table to one side of the room and laid his blanket down on the floor making sure to brush out any creases with his hand. Irabella laid hers down on the other side of the fire.

“Well, good night you two, try and get some sleep, we have a long journey tomorrow Irabella,” Mutana shouted as she walked up the stairs to Jariko’s room.

Jariko laid down on his blanket and looked up at the old wooden ceiling. He wanted to keep talking to Irabella, but he didn't know what to say or even why he wanted to talk. Usually he liked the quiet and didn't speak to anyone for longer than he needed to but she was different. There was something about her voice - even though most of the things she said were mean, the soft sound of her voice was addictive to Jariko. After ten long and excruciating minutes Jariko got the nerve to say something.

“So, why are you going to Orkestra as well? Are you gonna try and become the grandmaster too?” Jariko asked, not even sure if she was still awake. After a few moments passed and there was still silence, a disappointed Jariko rolled over onto his side to sleep.

Then, just as he was closing his eyes: “No, I'm not that powerful yet, I can barely use class two magic. I just owe a lot to Mutana and if she needs me during the competition I wanna be there to help. It sounds stupid but it's hard to explain to someone with no friends or family.”

This comment struck Jariko, but he knew she didn't mean it in a bad way.

“You're wrong, I do understand. Old man Rolo has done so much for me that if he ever needed my help there's nothing I wouldn't do and if I could've helped my mother to stop her dying I would have travelled over land and sea and battled any foe.”

Just the thought of this was enough to make Jariko tear up but the thought of what he described seemed to make Irabella chuckle.

“Well, I guess you do understand,” she said smiling as she rolled onto her side to look at Jariko, “Do you never take that tattered cloak off? It's probably better off outside to keep your horse dry.”

“It's a poncho and of course I do,” Jariko said, "It just means a lot to me and I don't know what I would do if something happened to it."

This seemed to quench Irabella’s curiosity for now but she still seemed a little suspicious, giving Jariko a look as she rolled over onto her back.

"So, what about you?" Jariko asked.

"What about me?"

"Why do you owe so much to Mutana?" He said, hoping to keep the conversation alive.

"She's the one who got me off the streets," she explained. "While I lived on the streets, the only way for me to get by was stealing, and I was pretty good at it, but the risk was too high so I broke into the church in my town and grabbed the first spell tome I found hoping I could learn something to help. It was for novice Manipulation magic. Took me almost a year to learn the most basic spell out of it but once I did, I got really good at it. Then one day I was trying to steal a coin purse from a nobleman who lived in my town. He was a bastard and didn't deserve to have so much, so I lifted his coin purse right out of his bag without a problem, grabbed it and tried to run, but someone grabbed my arm. It was one of the nobleman's bodyguards, he must’ve seen it float out of his bag and over to me and just as he was about to beat me, he froze and looked terrified. He started to flail around and shout, ‘where are you!?’ I didn't really understand what was going on, I thought he might've gone blind, or he was high. Next thing I know someone lifts me up and runs - it was

Mutana. She had seen everything and was so impressed by my skill with magic at such a young age she said it would've been a waste to have let me get beaten to death in the street. She later told me that she used class one magic to turn me invisible and that she was a new mage in town and as the newest priest she wanted a guide to show her around and she would teach me magic in return. That was four years ago now."

Jariko was stunned, he didn't really know what to say so he stayed silent trying to imagine what that must have been like to grow up like that. He then realised how privileged he had been; however similar their lives were in a lot of ways they couldn't be more different.

"I'm sorry that happened to you."

It was the only response Jariko could think of.

"I don't want or need your pity!" She snapped back. "I don't even know why I'm telling you all this, I've never told anyone that story before. Just leave me alone, I need to get to sleep."

Jariko was more than a little confused - he didn't really know what he had done to upset her so suddenly, but he thought it would be better not to ask any more questions or say anything at all and just go to bed. He would try to apologize in the morning. His mother was always in her best moods after breakfast so he thought Irabella might be the same. He rested his head down onto his arm and brought his knees to his chest like a dog curling up in its bed and drifted off to sleep.

It was the best night's sleep Jariko could remember having in a very long time. When he felt the warm rays of the sun touch his face, he slowly opened his eyes and stretched out on the floor. The fire had gone out and left black charcoal in its wake, but when Jariko looked past the fire to see Irabella still sleeping he was shocked to see that she had gone. He sat up and looked around the room hoping to see her sitting at the table but there was nothing - it was just Jariko in the motionless and silent room, just like every morning.

He jumped to his feet and ran upstairs hoping to see Mutana in his room but just like downstairs it was empty. He ran back downstairs missing most of the steps as he went and threw open the door almost ripping it off its hinges. As he looked out into the open field, he realised that they had left without him. He wasn't surprised, he never expected them to ask him to join them, but he wanted to at least say goodbye. This realisation broke Jariko's heart. He hadn't felt this kind of abandonment since his mother died. He turned around and walked back into the house, not knowing what to do with himself. He walked over to the shelves where he kept his food in the corner of the room to make some breakfast, but he found himself staring at the shelves. He turned around to walk upstairs but then he saw a note on the table. It was from Mutana. Jariko's hand moved before his mind even thought about it and started to read.

Dear Jariko,

Thank you so much for letting us stay at your house for the evening and being such a gracious host. I'm sorry that we have to leave so early but I have to meet someone in Rybalin and then be in Orkestra within a few days. It didn't seem right to wake you, you seemed so peaceful, but Irabella and I hope to get the chance to meet you again.

P.s. I know Irabella can be very intense, but she seems to like you, you didn't do anything wrong last night she just gets like that.

P.p.s. If you're sad that you didn't get to say goodbye, we are going to be in Rybalin until about midday today, so I hope you don't sleep in too late.

Mutana

His heart stopped and before he could take a breath he ran outside. Jariko couldn't afford a clock, but he never really needed one, he ate when he was hungry and slept when he was tired, but when knowing the time was important he would just look at the sun and take a guess. Today was not the day to be making guesses and assumptions, but he had no choice. He looked up at the sky and saw the blinding white sun. It wasn't too high in the sky, so it must've only been about nine 'o'clock, a grin crept onto Jariko's face.

He knew that if he skipped breakfast and left immediately, he could just make it before midday. He ran inside and packed as much as he could grab as quickly as his feet and hands could manage. He made sure to grab all the beetroot he had bought the day before and then ran back outside.

Runner was grazing in the field just like any other day but as if he could sense the beetroot his eyes darted over to Jariko who was holding the biggest piece of beetroot in the air, a second later Runner started to charge at him. At the same time Jariko began to charge as well on a collision course, neither seemed to be willing to slow down. Jariko started to run faster and faster and at the last second, he did a sharp turn to the left and headed south, Runner skidded to a stop, spun around on his hind legs and began to charge once again. The two were almost matched in speed but Runner was a margin faster and started to catch up. Just as they were neck and neck Jariko leapt high into the air, grabbing hold of Runner's mane and landing on his back. It was almost as if Runner was aware of the situation, and he just continued to run at full speed. The thought did pass through Jariko's mind that he might have finally broken his horse and Runner might never stop running but that wasn't a concern now, Jariko was determined that nothing was going to stop him getting to Rybalin by midday.

Chapter Six: Just in Time

It had been almost two hours give or take since Jariko left. He didn't have long and he could tell that Runner couldn't go on for much longer. He was beginning to get nervous that he would miss his chance to say goodbye.

If I miss them now, I might never see them again, he thought to himself. *I know they're going to Orkestra but could I really just up and leave, what about the house? Anyone could just claim it, that's all I have left of her.*

Thinking about his mother didn't help but the sickening feeling in his stomach was the same he used to feel all those years ago. It was inevitable that his mother would pop into his mind. This made it worse, but he didn't want to be alone again, he'd made two real friends and he didn't want to lose them too. Then an even worse thought came into Jariko's mind that was so much worse that he had to stop riding, he pulled Runner to a stop and dismounted.

What if they actually do ask me to come with them!?

He had been so preoccupied with getting to them he didn't think of what would happen if he actually made it in time. The real thought of leaving home caused a wave of panic and fear to run through his body. He knew that if Irabella asked him to come with them he wouldn't be able to say no so at this point Jariko had no idea what he actually wanted to happen. If he made it in time he would have to leave home, but if he didn't make it there in time he'd get to stay at home but he would never see Irabella again and he would be alone again.

This thought was tearing Jariko in half, but he heard a faint call on the wind in the direction he was heading. This surprised Jariko so much for a moment he completely forgot about everything else and focused on listening. He heard it again, but this time it sounded like a scream. Jariko jumped straight back on Runner and headed towards the sound. He heard a scream again, this time louder and more people were calling for help. A group of people started to appear on the horizon. As they got closer, Jariko realised they were running straight for him, so he rode to meet them.

"What's going on!?" He shouted but no one took any notice and continued running. A young woman ran up to Jariko and started frantically grabbing at him.

"Please help me!" was almost unintelligible through her shrill voice and cries, tears streaming down her face.

"What's happening?" Jariko asked the scared woman as he tried to calm her down. She gave up and began to run with the rest of the crowd once more.

"They are coming!" She shouted over her shoulder.

"Who!?" Jariko replied but his response fell on deaf ears. Everyone was so terrified by what had happened they almost didn't seem to notice Jariko standing in the road, then suddenly Jariko heard a familiar voice call out to him.

"Jariko!"

Jariko frantically looked around trying to find the source of the call when he spotted a familiar face in the distance.

"Old man Rolo!" He shouted out of excitement and relief. After a few minutes of dodging the frantic crowd Jariko reached Rolo who was comforting his crying wife.

"What is going on old man?" Jariko asked.

“Rybalin’s being attacked, my boy!” Rolo exclaimed.

“Attacked!? By who?”

“We didn't get a good look through all the smoke and panic, whoever it was, attacked at night and started setting fire to every house and cutting down anyone within arm’s reach. There was so much blood.”

This was unheard of in the west. Most attacks by other lands came from the south coast but there hadn't been an incident like that for a hundred years, and bandits would never attack such a fortified town like Rybalin. Then Jariko remembered the conversation he heard yesterday between the two men talking about the large group of armed mercenaries pretending to be merchants.

Could they be behind this!? Jariko thought. He was terrified of what he had to ask next.

“Old man, did you see two young women in town before you left? A human girl my age and an older Goblin, both in white robes?”

“Ah yes, bless the heavens they were there otherwise we wouldn't be talking to you now.”

“They protected you?” Jariko asked, relieved.

“Not just us, they are the ones who battled those demons while we all evacuated. The guards would have had no chance otherwise.” Rolo said a little prayer under his breath, thanking the Creators. “I don't know what we’ll do now!” Rolo said, trying to stay calm. “Our home and shop are gone, along with everything we owned,”

Rolo said. Rolo's wife let out a loud shrieking cry as he said this and Jariko could tell Rolo was holding back tears, trying to stay strong for his wife.

"I'm gonna go help the others!" Jariko said, "You two can head to my house - you can stay there. I'll send word of what happens when I can but whatever does happen, consider it yours, or at least until I get back. Keep it safe for me."

Jariko smiled as he said this. He had no problem leaving his house to Rolo and his wife. He knew that they would look after it for him. He didn't know what he was running into but whatever it was Jariko had a feeling it would be the start of a new life for him and at least this way he would have his home to come back to. This thought made it a lot easier to go after Irabella.

"Thank you Jariko, thank you," Rolo's wife said, tears still streaming down her face as she stretched onto her toes to give Jariko a hug.

"Yes, thank you my boy," Rolo said, grinning like his normal self again, "Consider your debt to me paid in full, and here, this might help." Rolo walked over to Jariko and Runner while pulling out something rolled up in a green leaf from the pouch strapped to his belt. It was no bigger than the palm of his hand and fed it to Runner.

"Take this, Runner," he said while patting Runner on the head. "It's like your medicine but a little more… instant. It will help."

He then untied the pouch and handed the whole bag to Jariko.

"You will need these more than me, just remember to only take one at a time and don't take it with your medicine, your heart might explode," Rolo said with a grin.

Just as Jariko was about to say thank you, Runner's eyes grew wide and his pupils shrank to a needle point and he recoiled onto his hind legs and let out a whinny. He bolted down the road so fast Jariko almost fell off his back. Jariko looked back and waved, seeing Rolo and his wife waving back as Runner charged towards the battle. It was like he was a demon who had been released from hell.

As Jariko approached the city he could see smoke climbing to the sky, Jariko's heart began to race.

"What am I doing!?" He thought, "I should turn back, but it's as if my body is moving by itself - I can't stop."

The thought of Irabella in trouble was too much. If something happened to her he would have nobody to blame but himself, so he kept charging into the unknown danger that lay ahead of him.

As he reached the city walls he pulled Runner to a stop in a thick screen of smoke and dismounted. As he did, he lost his balance and landed in the mud below him. Runner let out another whinny and bolted.

"Runner, come back!" Jariko shouted, raising a hand into the air towards his horse as he disappeared into the horizon. Then he noticed that the mud on his hands was a strange colour. Jariko slowly looked down at himself and saw that it wasn't just normal mud covering him, blood had turned the ground into a crimson sludge enveloping everything around him. Jariko stood up shaking, staring at his hands and then raising his head to look around, in a trance of fear and disbelief as he saw that the ground was littered with bodies, dozens of helpless people face down in the bloody mud, severed limbs around them and some were even disembowelled with their organs spread out on the floor where they lay. Jariko had never seen anything like it before.

"What...what monsters could do this?" He whispered, barely able to talk. He tried to steady himself but fell to the ground, retching and gagging until he finally threw up the last meal, he ate onto the blood soaked floor. He stayed there, staring at the ground trying to find a reason to run and never look back, then he suddenly heard a scream.

"Irabella!?" He shouted back but there was no answer. At this moment all the fear and terror melted away and turned into determination and focus. He picked himself up off the ground and sprinted through the wooden gate and entered the blazing city.

Chapter Seven: Unexpected Enemy

Charging in the direction of the scream, Jariko made his way through the city. The visibility was next to zero and the fire was out of control, but Jariko kept going. As he heard the scream again, closer this time, he ran a little further down the road until he saw a silhouette in the smoke.

"Irabella!?" He called.

"Where are you!?"

"Over here!" A voice replied. It was a woman's voice, but it wasn't Irabella. As he approached, she ran over to him stumbling and falling into his arms and onto the ground.

"My baby!" The women said, sobbing. "Please save my baby!" The women looked up at Jariko and he recognized her - she was the landlord at the Laughing Dragon Inn. Her name was Mrs. Barley and she had always been kind to Jariko.

"Where's your baby!?" He asked quickly.

"Inside the house," she said, pointing over to a half-fallen cabin. The door had collapsed and pulled some of the roof down with it.

"Stay here - I'll be right back," he said, rushing over to the cabin, looking for a way in. The fire had spread and surrounded the house making entry almost impossible. Coming up with the only plan he could think of, he climbed onto the neighbouring cabin's roof; it hadn't been consumed by the fire yet and the roof was still strong. He took a deep breath and started to run, then leapt into the air hoping to land on the roof of the collapsing building but fell straight through.

"That didn't work," he said to himself. Then, he heard crying from the small room at the back of the cabin. He ran over, opened the door, and there was the child sitting in a basket that had been made into a small bed. Jariko picked up the basket and headed for the hole he had just made in the roof. He looked around trying to find something he could stand on to reach the hole but nothing was tall enough.

This isn't good, Jariko thought. *I need to get this baby out of here or it's gonna die.*

Looking around for the slightest bit of inspiration he noticed one of the cabin's pillars holding the roof up was still standing. After assessing the situation, he surmised that if he broke the pillar it would create an opening that he could use to get out.

However, if it didn't work, he would just cause the cabin to collapse and fall onto him and the child, killing them both. He couldn't see another way. Clutching the basket tightly he readied himself and gave the pillar an almighty kick, breaking it in half. Jariko took some steps back and watched as a split second later a large section of the roof collapsed falling into one of the walls that then fell onto the fire making a small break in the ring of fire surrounding the house. Jariko ran for the opening holding tightly onto the basket just as the rest of the cabin started to fold in on itself and collapsed. Jariko took one more step then leapt out of the way just in time to see the cabin that only a few moments ago was standing turn into a pile of burning wood. Mrs.Barley ran over to Jariko crying with joy.

"Thank you so much, you saved my baby girl. Thank you!"

"Do you know the way out of here?" Jariko asked. She nodded, wiping the tears from her face with her sleeve and started to make her way to safety, still clutching the basket with her baby inside tightly. She suddenly stopped and turned back to Jariko.

"I think I heard shouting coming from further down the road, I think someone else needs help there too!" Jariko nodded back at her and she continued to run out of the city, Jariko turned to the direction she pointed and started running again.

Please be Irabella, please let me get there in time.

Jariko knew where he was in the city, recognising a few landmarks that were still standing. He was near the docks but then a thought occurred to him, he hadn't seen a single enemy yet, no one had tried to attack him. Was he too late? There was nothing to stop, just save whoever was left alive. Then suddenly he heard voices, but they weren't human, Goblin, or Elf and they didn't sound like any of the beast races - they were something else.

An acidic and scratchy voice said: "You had your fill yet?"

"I'm not done, these bones still have some meat left. Warm and bloody," replied the other creature.

"Well, hurry up, the rest of the pack has already left and the sun's becoming unbearable," the first creature said with a slight hiss in its voice. Jariko's heart sank to his stomach - the voices sounded unnatural and disformed and he did not want to meet them in person. But, curiosity got the better of him and he slowly crept to the closest cabin and peeked his head around the corner and what he saw would stick with him for life.

Standing surrounded by fire and death were two terrifying creatures that only belonged in books and tales, hunched over with large scales running from their brow over their head and down their backs and tail, long insect-like legs and standing on the balls of their feet with misshapen arms and two large pincers on either side of their mouths. The bigger one was standing, looking over at the other that was kneeling on the ground ripping bones from a body on the ground and pulling the meat off with its pincers. Jariko knew exactly what these creatures were. They were the same creatures he had seen on the way home the day before. They were the creatures in his mother's horror stories; they were the Roach-lins.

Jariko was paralysed with fear. They were everything his mother described in her scary stories she told Jariko as a child but to cause such devastation of this magnitude, they must be worse than the stories ever spoke of.

Should I attack them and find out why they did this? The bigger one did say that the rest have already left the city. I could definitely take one but maybe not both. I would most likely die.

Jariko stayed motionless for some time as he thought of every scenario and every way he might be able to survive a one on two battle with them. However the more he thought about it the less likely it seemed he'd survive, but it was crucial to get whatever information they had to the capital. If Roach-lins were attacking major cities, they might be planning something bigger. This could happen again in one of the other cities and those deaths would be Jariko's fault. He had to find out what they knew and try to stop them. As he was planning to split them up, the larger Roach-lin grabbed the other and threw him a few feet away.

"Enough, we need to find the others," he said, taking a few steps until he was standing over the other creature, still laying on his back.

"The others would've already taken those two witches to the boss by now and I don't wanna miss out on tearing their soft and delicious flesh from their pretty little bodies!"

Two witches!!? Did they really capture Mutana and Irabella!?

Jariko felt more terrified than he had been all day. He knew what he must do next.. He would have to follow these nightmarish creatures to wherever they lived and pray that his friends were still alive.

The two Roach-lins began to move. Strangely, they headed towards the market place - the market place was in the centre of the city, it wasn't an exit. As curious as this was, Jariko followed, being careful of the buildings collapsing around him and the fire that was still spreading from building to building.

It was sad to see the city in this way - Jariko had grown up here and this was the only other place he had ever been and could call home. As they made their way through town slowly walking and almost enjoying the view of anarchy, the Roach-lins began to talk once again. Jariko struggled to stay close enough to listen without getting caught, and after everything that had happened Jariko found himself becoming exhausted as he tried to keep up with them. His legs began to shake and his vision was becoming distorted. He fell against the wall of a cabin nearby and reached into his bag, pulling out his medicine. He hoped that an extra dosage would be enough to get him through the rest of the day and he took a large gulp from the bottle. He rested for a few moments and then he quickly began to feel better.

As he was putting the bottle back into his bag the smaller Roach-lins said: "Why did we even come here anyway?"

"Because we are looking for something the boss wants!" The other replied while stepping on a pile of dead villagers, almost as if he didn't know they were there.

"And what's he looking for then?" The smaller one replied.

"How would I know? I'm stuck here babysitting you!" The larger one said, annoyance in his voice.

"Well, did we find it?"

"I swear on Tando himself, if you ask me another question you will be burning with these putrid meat sacks!"

This comment surprised Jariko - he had never heard anyone swear on the Creator Tando before.

Tando? The trickster god? Do these things actually have the same gods as us?

Jariko's curiosity was becoming unbearable. That morning he didn't believe these things even existed, but now they were burning down villages and even had the same gods? While Jariko was deep in thought, he suddenly halted and realised that they were gone. They had just reached the open space where the market was held and disappeared. Jariko stayed amongst the cabins surrounding the marketplace, but he had lost sight of them. How could this be? He could see the cabins on the other side of the open area, and he'd been right behind them. He took a few steps forward and then he saw it - a huge gaping hole in the centre of the marketplace big enough to fit an ogre.

Is this how they got in? Jariko thought, trying to get a good look down the hole.

He walked over to a market stall that had collapsed and was still on fire. He broke off a panel of wood from the roof. Blowing on the flame, he walked back over to the hole and dropped the flaming wood in, he watched as it fell deeper and deeper illuminating the tunnel as it fell, until the light finally disappeared and was swallowed by the darkness.

It must be fifty feet deep at least, and could be even deeper, Jariko was more than a little alarmed at this realisation.

Is it even possible to live that far underground? If they do that's why no one knew they existed until now.

Jariko stood at the precipice of the hole. He was hoping that if he stood there long enough in the burning city centre some guards would show up, escort him home and tell him everything would be okay and that they would save his friends, but he knew no one would come.

There probably wasn't anyone for miles around, most likely heading for the aid and safety of Orkestra, but that was a two-day ride even at full speed so it would be almost a whole four days before anyone would be back here. By then the whole city would be just a memory, a pile of black ash representing what was once was a great city. Now it was only sadness and death, getting blown away in the wind. Irabella and Mutana were lost somewhere beneath, doomed to die in the dark void of the endless tunnels that could span most of Concorvia. Jariko was the only one who could help them, and he knew it.

I can't let them die, not now, not when I'm so close. Finding his courage, Jariko readied himself and picked up two pieces of pointed wood by his feet.

I can use these to climb down, he thought, banging them together to test their remaining strength. Then taking a deep breath he leapt, smashing into the shaft of the tunnel and stabbing the wood into the muddy wall. He then removed one of his handles and stabbed it back into the wall but lower than before. He was surprised this technique was working so well and began to make his way into the abyss.

Chapter Eight: Helpless

"Irabella!" A sweet voice called from a house at the top of the hill. "Dinner's ready!"

A child appeared from the thistles with a wooden sword in one hand and a doll in the other.

"Coming mother!" Replied the young girl. She began to run up the hill towards the voice calling her name, swinging the toy sword back and forth in front of her, making whooshing and clanking noises as she did so. But, the young girl realised the more she ran, the further away the house on the hill became.

"Irabella!" The voice called again, more frantic and alarmed than before.

"Mother! Where are you mother?!" The young girl cried as the house was lost in the distance. All of a sudden the young girl heard growling noises from behind her, then out of the thick bushes and thistles a horrific creature jumped out and began to chase her. The young girl screamed and ran blindly into the open fields to get away. The sky began to turn black and the heavens opened up into a downpour of rain and lightning. The young girl was horrified until she heard her name again.

"Irabella!"

The young girl ran towards the voice as it grew louder and louder.

"Bella! Irabella!"

The voice was coming from just over the hill but the creature was still chasing her. She ran as fast as she could and as soon as she reached the peak of the hill she realised there was a gaping hole in the ground but she was moving too fast to stop and she fell, plummeting down into the void of darkness.

"Bella! Bella!"

Suddenly, Irabella awoke sitting up in a daze, confused about what had just happened until she realised it was a dream.

"Bella, thank the Creators you're okay." It was Mutana. She was kneeling next to Irabella leaning over and hugging her. The light above her was blinding, and Irabella closed her eyes and rubbed them as they adjusted.

"Where are we?" She asked, squinting, trying to look at Mutana.

"I'm not sure, it seems like we're underground, those things must have brought us here," she said standing up and holding her hand out for Irabella. Irabella took it and stood up feeling a sharp pain in her ribs, recoiling in pain as she grabbed her side.

"What happened? I thought we were winning?" Irabella asked.

"We were, but I don't think they were trying to kill us, otherwise we would be dead already," Mutana said. She continued, "One of them snuck up on you and hit you so hard in the back you fell to the ground then it hit you again around the head. As soon as I turned my back to try to help you the same thing happened to me. I get the feeling that they were in control the whole time, just waiting for the right moment to strike."

"But why bring us here?" Irabella replied, rubbing her eyes once again.

"You got me. But now you're awake we can start trying to find a way out of here."

Irabella was beginning to make out her surroundings and understand the situation better. They were in a prison, but unlike any human prison. The whole thing was just a pit in the ground. The roof of the cell was open but covered by bars that looked like bones. They were held together by rope made of what looked like hair.

There were two blankets thrown on the ground and a wooden bucket on the other side from where Irabella was sitting, the walls were just dirt and rock and so was the ground, horrid and dirty with worms and other insects. It was the simplest prison Irabella had ever seen or had the displeasure of being stuck in but nevertheless it was effective. The bars didn't need to be strong if you couldn't reach them.

"Any ideas on how we are going to get out of here?" Irabella asked.

"I'm not even sure where 'here' is to be truthful. When they were dragging us, I woke up for a few seconds and I saw we were in a cave or maybe a tunnel before one of those things hit me again. My guess is we're in underground tunnels." Mutana explained as she stretched out her arms to grab the bars that were obviously well out of reach.

"Why don't you use your magic to get us out?" Irabella asked sitting down against the muddy wall.

"The thought did cross my mind, but if we are underground, using my magic could quickly burn up whatever breathable air is down here and the heat could cause a sudden shift in air pressure that might even cause an explosion, blowing everything in this cave to cinders, including us. It would be smarter to wait until we understand our situation better and look for an opportunity," Mutana explained.

She was best at the use of Class five magic - Fabrication - in the form of fire, an extremely powerful form of magic but equally destructive, and in a lot of cases throughout the history of magic, this magic form had killed the caster when not used carefully.

"What about you? Do you feel strong enough to lift those bars off the top?" Mutana asked.

Irabella nodded, stood up and shook her arms and cracked her neck. At her level, the strength of her magic was equal to her own physical strength. She lifted both her arms above her head and closed her eyes. A few seconds later the bars began to shake and rattle but just as the bars began to slowly lift in the air a ferocious beast slammed down on the bars with an unnaturally elongated arm. The long claws and leather-like pads on its front foot pinned the bars back down. Then from the shadows it crept forward and stared down at them growling viciously. They both recoiled in fear and dread as they realised what guarded their prison. It was a Hellina.

A hellish creature with unnaturally long limbs for climbing rocky Mountains, trees and catching prey, it had the face of a wolf but twice the size with brown bristle-like fur with orange spots. The two sorceresses were speechless as the realisation of their doom became more apparent.

"Are we gonna die?" Irabella asked as she turned to Mutana, trying to hide the fear in her voice. Mutana turned and pulled Irabella into her arms.

"It's going to be alright, they have kept us alive for this long. Let's just hope their reason for not killing us doesn't disappear." As she said this, they started to hear voices approaching.

“Get that thing outta here before it eats another prisoner!” The Roach-lin commanded. They could hear chains rattling and claws scratching at rock as the Hellina was dragged away, then they saw two orange eyes peer over the edge and looked down at them, their pincers snapping at the fine air and making an unnerving sound that filled them with fear.

“You ready to meet the boss?” The Roach-lin said before making a noise like it had started choking, but by the look on its face it was laughter. “You're really gonna like him.”

The eyes darted off and suddenly the bars were dragged away and an old rotting rope was thrown down the hole. Irabella glanced at Mutana, her face uneasy with worry as they were both still uncertain why they were there. Irabella had a feeling they would soon be finding out why they were so fortunate not to be dead.

They climbed out of the pit and found themselves in a large cave-like room with dozens of pits just like the one they had just left. Some with the bars still covering the opening.

"*There must be other poor souls trapped in those,*" Irabella thought.

"*Maybe we aren't special. Maybe that's why they attacked Rybalin: to get slaves. But why go through so much effort just for a handful of slaves*?" Irabella contemplated.

There were pieces to this puzzle she didn't understand, hiding the big picture from her. while she was deep in thought the guards walked them over to the exit of the large room and pointed at the ground.

"You stay here!" The guard said in a gurgling voice, proceeding to walk over to another pit and pull the bars off and throw another rope in. Four other guards copied these actions on the remaining pits and all the other prisoners were shepherded over to where Irabella and Mutana were standing and filtered into a line.

"What do you think happens now?" Irabella whispered, but before Mutana could respond one of the guards banged a club made of bone and rock on the wall of the cave.

"No talking!" He snarled, then turned his attention back to the other prisoners. Once the rest had been rounded up, they bound their hands with the same rotting rope they'd climbed out of the pit with and started to escort them all through the exit and down a long tunnel, it was clear that they were indeed deep underground and it wouldn't be easy to get out of. Even if they found a way to escape, they might not be able to find a way out. There might not even be a way out.

The tunnel seemed endless with detours and other tunnels heading in other directions. There wasn't any light apart from the torch the guard at the front was holding to light the way through the labyrinth of tunnels. They definitely were not going to get out without help. Eventually they came to a large open space. The walls were riddled with little holes and ladders leading up to each one.

"*This must be where they live*!" Irabella thought trying to get a look inside one of them, her curiosity was getting the best of her. She hadn't thought about what they had discovered, but these creatures had not been seen in an age and they were walking through these expansive tunnels and architecture that they had never seen before. The tunnels could be all over Concorvia, little colonies dotted around and living all this time right under their feet. This thought truly stunned Irabella. If she survived this it would be the greatest discovery since the Gnomes in the north. She didn't have much time to be entranced by this thought, however, for they had finally arrived at what could only be described as the inside of a palace, dirty and rudimentary, but still large and breath-taking.

It was a large room, square in shape and with large steps decreasing in size until they reached an open area in the centre like some kind of colosseum. However, Irabella didn't get the sense there would be a fight; it felt more like an execution. Just like all the other rooms and tunnels, this colosseum had been dug out and the walls were made up of rock and mud however it seemed to have droplets of water falling from the ceiling. This was strange to Irabella.

"*Are we under a body of water!? Could all this be under the west coast sea!*?" She thought and wondered if it would be possible to have that much weight above them.

It didn't seem to have much structural support apart from large vines that crawled up the corners of the room. Irabella kept note of this and continued into the colosseum. They started to make their way down the stairs. The large fire pits and torches scattered through the room gave more than enough light to see the way to the centre.

The sound of hissing and the vicious tapping of pincers filled the room as an army of Roach-lins watched in what seemed like excitement. They reached the centre and were all made to kneel on the ground. This gave Irabella a good chance to see all the other prisoners and that's when the truth became a little clearer and more than a little horrific. All the prisoners were women -

human, Goblin and Elf women had all been taken, but there were no men.

She looked over at Mutana and the look on her face made it obvious she was thinking the same thing. It was at this moment Irabella truly felt afraid and helpless, made all the worse with flashbacks of her childhood and the last time she felt like this. She promised herself all those years ago that she would never feel this way again, she would rather die than be helpless. She wanted to jump up and start fighting, she would certainly die but it would be better than whatever they were planning on doing to her. It would just be a case of how many of these things she could take with her and as satisfying as the thought was she couldn't move if she wanted to; her body refused to take action. Then, almost out of nowhere, a large thud shook the ground beneath them. Then, it shook again.

"*Footsteps*!?" She thought staring at a darkened corridor at the other end of the arena. They continued getting closer and closer until a shrivelled and long-fingered hand crept out of the shadows of the passage and grabbed the wall as a Roach-lin stepped out. It was not like the others. This one was three times the size, had six eyes, two sets of pincers, legs like a horse and not just two arms but two other handless pairs of appendages hanging from its waste.

The crowd let out an almighty roar as it entered the colosseum. Then, Irabella remembered what the guard had said when they released them - this thing must be the king in this place. The one they had called "the Boss".

Chapter Nine: Lost in the Dark

Jariko felt like it had been hours since he had climbed down the hole and into the tunnels. It was a lot deeper than he had imagined and he had lost the trail of the two Roach-lins he was following a while ago. As he was aimlessly walking through the labyrinth, he had used the fire he threw down the hole as a torch, but it went out. The only light remaining was the odd torch stuck in the walls at every junction of the tunnels. There was a horrid smell coming from somewhere, but Jariko couldn't figure out what it was or where it was coming from. At every junction he made sure to take the path that smelt less vile. The walls were damp and muddy as he ran his fingers along the edges to find his way in the darkness and the ground crunched every time, he took a step.

He tried not to think about what he was stepping on, but he had a good idea judging from the sound and smell that they were the remains of animals, lining the tunnels with bones. Jariko had no idea what to do or where to go. Even if he found Irabella and Mutana, could he find his way back or climb out the way he had come in? This was a question he didn't want to think about because he already knew the answer, but he marched on despite this.

Another few hours passed, and it didn't seem like he had even made a dent in discovering all the tunnels. He was truly lost and hadn't seen a light for way too long, until at last as he came around a corner. There in the distance, a light was shining. Brighter than the torches he had seen on the way, he didn't know what it was but it would definitely be useful to him in one way or another.

Jariko silently made his way towards the light and once he got close enough he was able to make out horrid voices coming from a room that the light was coming from and he knew it was more Roach-lins.

"I can't believe we're stuck here looking after these oafs. We're gonna miss what they do to all the prisoners. Everyone's in the main chamber already," one of them said. "These things are too dumb to break out anyway, why don't we sneak off and watch what happens? No one will know we even left. The boss will be too preoccupied," he continued.

Both let out a shrieking cackle as they left their posts and disappeared into the darkened tunnel ahead. This was the luckiest thing that had happened to Jariko that day. He crept forward, still staying quiet just in case there were more around and as he turned into the lit room he was shocked at what he saw - twelve hulking Ogres locked up in cages with bars as thick as tree trunks and surrounding a large fire pit filled with bones and burning flesh.

Jariko had heard stories of the Ogres, but truly underestimated their size and intimidating presences.

The Ogres are from the Giant race also known as the Kigatos. As the name implies they are giant in size, and the prominent species stand at almost twelve feet tall, with four arms, long hair and are as strong as ten men. They are a primitive race, hailing from the south-east across the river in their country which is also named Kigatos. The Ogres, however, are said to be even more primitive than normal Giants. You can have a full conversation with the Giants of the south, but Ogres are said to hardly know any words and are too dumb to understand any form of civilisation.

At some point in history the tribes of the Giants were all the same but one tribe decided to head north to Deuterra, over the river and across the vast landscapes. No one knows why they decided to do this but we do know decades ago, a group of travellers found a mountain swarming with Giants but different to any they had seen.

These Giants were hairless and had developed the method of walking on all fours like a gorilla. This caused their backs to arch, making them shorter at ten feet tall. Their two sets of arms, normally one pair above the other had moved so both pairs sat on their shoulders. This was most likely due to them walking on their secondary pair of hands like gorillas and making them more dominant. The other pair of arms don't seem to be used for much apart from fighting and showing dominance. This has led scientists and mages alike to argue about whether they can be classed as quadrupeds but no one seems to have a definitive answer. Due to evolving in such a drastic way that they barely resemble their Kigatos cousins, they were given a new name and henceforth known as Ogres, meaning king of the mountains.

This must be how they dig these tunnels, Jariko thought, slowly walking around the room staring at the Ogres, taking every detail of the creatures in, however they didn't seem aggressive towards him, they just stared back at him. They seemed to sense something familiar about him. Or, on second thought, maybe they just hated their Roach-lin masters and were friendly to any other race they saw. Jariko approached one and their eyes locked on one another. He knew they most likely wouldn't understand him if he asked them anything but after the day he'd had, any form of conversation was much desired.

"Hello big guy, my name is Jariko," he said, pausing and waited to see if there was anything that suggested the creature understood. After a few moments he continued, "How long have they kept you here? Must be sad being away from your mountains."

The creature's eyes became sad and as terrifying as these creatures were Jariiko pitied them.

"Wanna help me get my friends outta here? You can come too?" Jariko wanted to open the cage and let the Ogres out, but from the stories he had heard they would probably kill him. No matter how docile they seemed, Jariko didn't trust them - they were still basically animals after all.

"Well, I'll come back for you guys when I can," Jariko said with a large smile and began to walk away. Just as he was about to enter the tunnel once again he heard a deep and ominous voice that spoke out to him.

"Giants, friends."

Jariko froze in disbelief. He spun around and ran back to the Ogre.

"Y..you can talk?!" Jariko exclaimed. No one had ever heard of an Ogre talk before.

"We talk good, just not much to say to small people," the Ogre explained. This comment amazed Jariko - they could talk all this time, but just didn't feel the need to.

"So, why talk to me?" Jariko asked.

"We trapped, you help," the ogre said, struggling to find the words. Jariko nodded and grabbed hold of the latch that held the cage door shut, but stopped and stared at the ogre again. A little part of him still thought they might kill him and escape, even if they could talk.

"Trust Bombo," the ogre said, pressing both his massive fists on his chest softly. This seemed like a gesture of friendship. Jariko copied the gesture and proceeded to release the Ogre.

"So, your name is Bombo?" Jariko asked, still in disbelief. Bombo nodded then pointed at the other Ogres.

"You save friends, we help save friends," Bombo said with an unsettling smile. This made Jariko uncomfortable, but nevertheless he did as the Ogre asked. At this point he didn't plan to even survive, let alone save Irabella and Mutana, but with the help of the Ogres it seemed possible. He released the other Ogres who all put their fists onto their chests and chanted: "Jabo, Jabo."

Jariko didn't understand what they were saying.

He turned to Bombo and asked, "What does Jabo mean?"

Bombo laughed, "You Jabo"

Jariko didn't understand at first then he realised it must be his name in their language. Jariko accepted this fact quickly - he had never been given a nickname before and this strangely made him a little giddy. They weren't the terrible and dangerous abominations he had been led to believe by his mother - they were friendly and honourable.

"Do you know where they keep prisoners?" Jariko asked.

"Bombo knows, but if Jabo wanna find friends he go to big room," Bombo began to walk into the tunnel and point in the direction the two guards walked. Jariko didn't completely understand what he meant, but followed Bombo down the tunnel. The Ogres could only just fit in the tunnels but seemed to know exactly where they were going.

"Did you dig these tunnels?" Jariko asked, wanting to confirm a suspicion he had.

"Bombo digs tunnels for bugs," he said, changing direction down another tunnel. "We dig long time, makes Bombo tired."

“Why don't you just escape? You could probably kill all of them, big guy," Jariko said patting Bombo’s back. He did it without thinking then realised and pulled his hand back. Bombo didn't seem bothered by it; he was distracted trying to remember the way.

"Some try but bugs have strong magic. Giants strong and put up fight but magic stronger." This seemed to upset Bombo as he said it. He must have lost friends to the Roach-lins."But you smart. You make plan, we leave and return to mountain," Bombo said. This didn't fill Jariko with confidence. He didn't even know Roach-lins could use magic and now he had to fight them. At that point Jariko stopped asking questions and followed Bombo. He was deep in thought about how they would get out of this alive, and how was he going to fight a whole colony of Roach-lins. If even the Ogres were no match for them, what could he do to defeat them? Any fights he had gotten into in his young life were simple to win - he just had to hit them harder. But this strategy wasn't going to work, not this time.

A little time had passed and they suddenly heard a deafening roar. It echoed through the tunnels and made Jariko’s stomach sink in fear.

"That sounded like thousands of them," Jariko said.

"Boss here," Bombo replied. Jariko remembered hearing the two in Rybalin mention a Boss.

"Is he trouble?" Jariko asked.

"Bigger than Bombo," said Bombo. That comment shook Jariko to his core.

"Bigger than Bombo?! This is a nightmare," Jariko said to himself.

As they approached a bright light at the end of the tunnel, Jariko's heart began to race. They could hear talking but it didn't sound like the Roach-lins in Rybalin. This one had a voice like scraping metal. It resonated in their ears and sent a chill down Jariko's spine. They crept forward just enough to see the colosseum shaped room in all its glory. Hundreds of Roach-lins were looking down into the centre where twelve women were kneeling on the floor with their hands bound.

"There they are! My friends!" Jariko whispered, pointing in excitement, trying not to alarm anyone. Bombo pointed back down to the centre - in his delight Jariko hadn't noticed the eleven foot monstrosity lurking over the women, but once he did all the colour drained from Jariko's face.

"That's Boss," Bombo explained, not looking much better than Jariko.

The thought of running was in his head, abandoning his friends and escaping with Bombo while they were all distracted. It would be their best chance of escape. Jariko leant on the wall of the tunnel and slid down until he was sitting on the ground with his head between his knees.

"Plan Jabo, we attack now or die!" Bombo insisted.

Jariko's mind was running too quickly to think straight.

Should they run? Should they attack? Could they save everyone or would they all die? Just as he was spiralling into madness, a droplet of water fell from the ceiling and right onto the tip of Jariko's nose.

"Water?" He said out loud.

"From lake," Bombo said pointing up.

"We're beneath the lake of Agorith?" Jariko said, his surprise making his words burst out loudly and he had to cover his mouth. It had felt like he had walked for miles, because he had - almost thirty miles east of Rybalin. Then Jariko realised he had never been this far from home before. His mother always wanted to see the great lake but they could never make the journey. He looked around the room and after a few minutes Jariko smiled and all the panic and worry melted away.

He turned to Bombo and the other Ogres and said, "I have a plan."

Chapter Ten: The Plan

The roar of the crowd was deafening as the Boss made his way to the centre of the room. They didn't stop until the Boss put his insect-like hand into the air and shouted:

"SILENCE!"

The ground shook ever so slightly and the room fell silent. Nothing happened for a few moments and not a sound could be heard apart from drops of water. The Boss began to step towards the imprisoned women. The creaking and cracking sound of his outer shell was unsettling.

"Who out of you can talk?" His voice was shrill and dry. He leaned in and stared into the eyes of one of the women. "Or are you all too scared?" The crowd burst into a cackle of laughter and tapping of pincers.

"Let me introduce myself. I am the Boss around here, but my name is Blata. We don't usually entertain guests but what my Queen asks of me… I do."

"Queen?" Irabella said, shocked at herself for speaking.

"Ahhhh, so one of you can talk." He took three long and heavy steps over to Irabella and leant in. He seemed to smell her then, his pincers tapping faster than before almost like a rattle.

"And you're a witch from Ferradon?" He asked. Irabella's eyes widened. "Do not be surprised, young witch, every meatbag from that cesspool reeks of the gutter, and the residue of magic lingers around you."

This comment struck a nerve with Irabella and she snapped back, "Who's this queen of yours? I thought you were the Boss, but I guess you're just another lacky who takes orders." At this point Irabella's mouth was moving by itself and she was just as shocked as everyone else, even though she had a stern look on her face. Blata let out a quiet hiss as he stood up straight and burst into laughter.

"I like you," he said pointing at Irabella and chuckling, then just as quickly, his laughter stopped. "Back to the business at hand." His nightmarish face turned serious as he began to scan the women that kneeled in front of him.

"Word of a criminal woman near my colony has reached my ears and I have been tasked to find her and take her to my Queen for further…" he paused, "Interrogation." Blata began to walk among the women smelling them, tapping his pincers as he did so.

"I have not been told much but I do know she is a thief and has powers over the less wise versions of your races. She goes by the name Sireana." He grabbed one of the women by the hair and lifted her into the sky. She let out a scream from the intense pain, and Irabella could almost feel the agony. Blata began to swing the woman around like a dead rabbit, showing off the control he had to all of the other women.

"If you are here Sireana, please come forward now. You're too smart to try and escape. You probably think there is a way out of this. Just save me the time. If you do, I will only kill most of the women here. I'm sure all my beautiful swarms are hungry. The others will simply be used for... nesting."

The crowd once again roared in excitement. This broke some of the women's spirits. A few started to uncontrollably sob into the dirt, eyes glazed over in fear. One woman couldn't take it and tried to run before Blata gave a nod and three Roach-lins pounced on her. As they sank their razor-sharp pincers into her skin, Irabella shut her eyes so she didn't have to see what was going to happen. Just as she did, a figure exploded out from the shadows, grabbing a large rock and in one swift motion span, throwing it with such force the impact was enough to kill all three Roach-lin as they were standing over the helpless woman. The figure charged forward and stopped in between the woman and the Roach-lins closest to her. The room was deathly silent until Irabella opened her eyes slowly and in disbelief she realised who the figure was.

"Jariko!" She shouted, unable to control her excitement. A smile crept onto Mutana's face.

"I told you to meet us at midday," Mutana said, grinning.

"Yeah, sorry I'm late. Thanks for waiting for me," Jariko said standing straight, puffing out his chest trying to hide his terror.

"And who might you be? My swarm made sure they killed all the guards," Blata said, taking a few steps cautiously towards Jariko. By this point every Roach-lin in the hall was standing and waiting, frothing at the mouth in anger.

"My name's Jariko. I was just passing through and noticed you accidently picked up two of my friends so I'm just here to take them home. I'll take all the others while I'm here too."

Blata erupted with laughter and waved his hands to tell his swarm to sit back down.

"What makes you think I would let you take them? Because, if you haven't noticed, I'm in charge around here and no one leaves without my say." Blata said, taking a few more steps closer to Jariko. "And you... do not... have my say."

Jariko and Blata stood a few feet from one another and stared each other down. Jariko's heart was racing and he was struggling to breath properly, taking small and quick breaths. Then, in a moment of tranquillity, he calmed himself down and took a deep breath, looked around the room and smiled.

"I don't need you to agree, I'm leaving with these women," he said calmly, trying to seem threatening.

"How do you think you're gonna do that? Does a kid like you really think you can fight all of us at once?" Blata sneered as every Roach-lin stood up and began tapping their pincers.

"No, but that was never the plan…"

A moment later Bombo and seven other Ogres erupted out from the tunnel charging through the crowds of Roach-lins like twigs. As they swung their massive arms back and forth swatting them like flies, putrid yellow blood flew through the air splattering on the walls and coming down like rain. Simultaneously Jariko ran forward, grabbed hold of one Blata's large pincers, launched into the air vaulting over him and landing on his back. Jariko grabbed the other pincer and pulled. It made him feel like the bull riders in the circus that came to Rybalin. Blata swung back and forth jumping and clawing at Jariko, but due to his size and shape, he couldn't reach Jariko. Jariko was safe as long as he could hold on.

It took a few minutes for the Roach-lins to get over the surprise and begin to counterattack. This was the first time Jariko saw the Roach-lins use magic and it was a sight to see. The ground and walls seemed to come alive as vines from all over crept out from beneath the dirt like snakes attacking their prey, wrapping around the Ogre's legs and impaling one through his shoulder. The Ogres tried to break the vines but every time they broke one, two more took its place. Pulling the Ogres down into the ground, Jariko looked around in the panic and chaos and noticed a group of Roach-lins waving their hands gracefully through the air as if they were painting a picture in their mind; the Roach-lin mages were using their magic to subdue the Ogres. Jariko, still on the Blata's back, shouted to Irabella and Mutana who were busy untying the other women amongst the battle.

"Bella! There!" Jariko said nodding at the small group. She nodded back and ran over to Mutana and they spoke for a few moments. Jariko couldn't make out what they were saying but a second later Mutana ran towards the Roach-lins. They were almost at the top of the room and Mutana was still in the centre, there was no way she would make it before all the Ogres were dead, but suddenly she leapt and took off from the ground. Jariko was amazed she could jump so high. She was soaring over the battle and releasing a thin stream of orange and red fire from her mouth, scorching a line of Roach-lins and then the group of mages before landing at the top of the room. It didn't look natural.

There's no way she's that agile, that's impossible! Jariko thought until he looked back at Irabella who had her hand up in the direction Mutana had just run. Then it clicked in his head. Irabella was lifting her into the air and with the momentum from the run she had started to fly. Jariko was impressed by their skill and quick thinking.

However, while he was distracted a Roach-lin came up from behind him and jumped onto Blata's back knocking Jariko off, but in the process Jariko pulled out one of Blata's pincers as he fell to the ground with a mighty thud. Blata screamed in pain sounding like a dying animal. Before Jariko could get up, Blata was standing over him slamming one of his sharp clawed feet onto Jariko's chest, pinning him to the ground.

"I'll kill you for this," Blata said snarling in anger while yellow goo seeped out of the wound on his mouth. It dripped on Jariko's arm and he could feel it sting his skin. Jariko tried to get up but as he did Blata pointed his sharp claws down and stomped again, stabbing them into Jariko's shoulders. He yelled in pain. They didn't go deep but it was the most severe pain Jariko had ever felt. Blata began twisting his foot back and forth, his claws slowly making their way deeper into Jariko's shoulders. The pain was too much and Jariko had no choice but to speed up the plan. He wanted to wait until all of the Ogres had made their way to the centre of the room, but he would die if he didn't act now.

Amidst screams and groans of pain Jariko shouted, "Now, now, do it now!"

Nothing happened for a few moments and Jariko's heart sank as he thought his plan had failed, but then he heard the shout of the other four Ogres that weren't in the fight.

While the battle was going on, the four Ogres had made their way around the tunnels to each corner of the great hall and climbed to the roof that was held up by enormous vines, creeping up the walls and spreading out along the roof. Jariko realised that they must be holding the roof up, in such a big room under the weight of all the water above it would need some kind of support. All four of the Ogres roared as they pulled on the enormous vines, their arms throbbing and veins popping as they used every ounce of strength they had.

Then as if pulling a carrot from a garden, the vines pulled out from the wall and the Ogres swung off them like chimps before letting go and falling to the ground with a loud thud. The whole room stopped, shocked, and watching in terror as the roof began to crumble.

A moment later every Roach-lin ran for their lives climbing over each other, some getting trampled as they filtered into the tunnels like rats. Jariko was overwhelmed with triumph knowing his plan had worked. He was so happy for a moment he forgot about the pain but was quickly reminded as Blata leant in digging his claws deeper and roaring in Jariko's face. The smell of his breath was what you would imagine a rotting corpse would smell like. He raised his hand and just as he was about to strike Jariko with a deadly blow, a large boulder fell from above, striking him on his back and knocking him forward and onto Jariko. Jariko rolled Blata away and used this chance to stumble to his feet and struggling to walk he dragged himself over to Blata. He stood over him for a few moments and stared. Blata was stuck on his back clawing at the air and trying to tap his remaining pincer. Then with one swift motion, he lifted his foot and stomped down with enough force onto Blata's head to stop the wiggling and the massive, disfigured body became limp. Jariko took a few deep breaths, put the large pincer that was still in his hand in his pocket and stumbled over to Irabella and Mutana.

"Are you okay?!" Irabella asked, trying to check Jariko's wounds. Jariko stepped back recoiling as if she was going to make it worse somehow.

"I'll be fine, we just need to get out of here!"

"Okay then, so what's the plan now?" Mutana asked eagerly awaiting his response.

"I don't know," Jariko replied, grabbing his left shoulder, which was the worse of the two wounds.

"What do you mean, you don't know?!" Irabella shouted.

"I didn't think we would survive this far."

Just as Jariko said this, Bombo charged over and scooped Jariko up into his arms.

"You save friends, we save friends." Bombo said smiling. Jariko looked confused but then, as if synchronised, all the Ogres ran out and grabbed one woman each and huddled in the centre of the room.

“Hold breath,” Bombo said just before the roof collapsed. A torrent of water flooded the main hall and down onto the group of Ogres.

It was disorientating as they were thrown around by the tides of water. The water was too muddy to see what was happening and the stress of the weight of the water was almost too much. Jariko tried desperately to stay conscious but the pain of his wound and the beating from the water was too much and he began to get tunnel vision before passing out completely.

It was dark for a moment before Jariko could see something in the distance. He began to walk toward the figure. Once he got closer he realised it was his mother, waiting for him and smiling, holding her arms out just like every night when Jariko returned from playing in the woods. Tears welled up in Jariko’s eyes as he ran and leaped into his mother's arms. The two were silent, enjoying each other's embrace before his mother spoke.

“Well done, my little hero. You’re all grown up.”

Jariko pulled away and looked into his mother's eyes, holding back the tears.

“I'm sorry I couldn't protect you Mum, I miss you so much.” He said as she leant down and brushed a tear from his cheek with one of her fingers.

“I don't need protection anymore my love, but you have new friends who need you to protect them, it's time for you to go now,” she said, smiling and kissing him on the forehead. As she began to suddenly become further and further away, Jariko started running, desperately trying to reach her while tears streamed down his face.

Jariko reached out his hand and said, "MUM! PLEASE!"

Jariko sprung up, coughing up water. He was on the beach of a lake. It must've been evening because the sun was setting. He sat there silently staring at the sunset as the orange glow reflected off the lake and showing a sky on fire.

"Jabo lives," Bombo shouted, beating his chest. Jariko looked around and saw Irabella, Mutana and Bombo standing around him. It took a few moments to realise where he was and what had just happened.

"We survived?!" Jariko exclaimed, failing to hide his excitement and disbelief.

"Mostly," Mutana said sadly, pointing further down the beach.

Jariko turned his head and on the shore of the water he saw the corpse of an Ogre and a young woman. Two of the women were sitting over her lifeless body and were weeping uncontrollably. He thought they must've been sisters judging from their similar looks.

"And we are still missing another pair, we think they might've gotten trapped in the tunnels." Irabella explained, wiping a tear from her face with her sleeve.

Jariko couldn't speak. The deaths of these people weighed on his mind, tearing all of the excitement away.

“It's my fault, I killed them... I... I should’ve thought of a better plan,” Jariko said. He tried to hold back the tears but they overcame him. He began to sob and hide his head in his hands.

“If you hadn't saved us, we would all be dead,” Mutana said wrapping her arms around him.

“And we dig for long time and you free us. Gobo and Tuba chose to fight. They die happy. They die free,” Bombo said, sincerity in his voice. These words did helped Jariko cope and he nodded his head, but the feeling of guilt still bore down on him and he continued crying.

They all sat on the beach and watched as the sun disappeared into the horizon. Once the sun had set and night took its place, a group of the survivors built a small fire from broken sticks and leaves on the beach. Mutana clicked her fingers and a small flame sparked into existence at the tip of her finger. She held it under a leaf and as it lit up she dropped it on the pile of dead sticks and a fire grew. The other group buried the body of the Ogre and the young women in the sand, using their hands and large rocks to carve the ground away to make two shallow graves. As the others set up camp, two of the women who survived were so damaged by the last few hours that all they could do was continue to sit in the sand and stare blankly into the empty space, glassy eyed and shivering.

Once this was done, everyone said a prayer and they all tried to sleep.

"Do you think they will be okay?" Jariko whispered over the fire, gesturing to the women.

"If they're lucky, in a few weeks they might get over it," Mutana explained.

"And if they are not lucky?" Jariko replied.

"They're probably gonna be like that for the rest of their lives. Something like this can cause people to lose their minds. Yesterday they were buying and selling fruit and vegetables, then a few hours later almost getting eaten by a creature they didn't know existed. It can mess up normal people, but we are different!" Mutana said sitting up to look Jariko in the eyes. "Me and Irabella are fighters and after today you showed us that you are too." She raised a finger to point at him trying to solidify her point.

"But I couldn't save everyone," Jariko replied, choking on his tears, not wanting to cry in front of her again.

"Do you really think if anyone else followed us down there they could've done what you did? You befriended twelve Ogres who are supposed to be savages and went head to head with an eleven-foot cockroach. Trust me Jariko, you're a hero. Now get some sleep. We have a big day tomorrow."

"We do?" Jariko said.

"Yeah, you're taking us to Orkestra. I'm hiring you as my bodyguard and I'm not taking no for an answer." She laid back down and immediately seemed to fall to sleep. Jariko didn't know how to react to this. He wanted to scream with happiness but his guilt quickly flooded his mind once again and the two feelings fought in his head.

He continued to sit on the beach by the fire and think about everything he could've done differently and stewed in his own guilt well into the night. He couldn't help but feel responsible for the deaths. He never even spoke to any of them, but their lives were his responsibility and he failed them. In his anger and frustration, Jariko picked up a sharp rock that was laying beside him, stumbling to his feet clutching his shoulder as he walked over to the water's edge.

He put the rock against the palm of his hand and sliced his palm open. He clenched his fist tight and the blood seeped through his fingers and dripped into the water, tears in his eyes Jariko spoke, "With my blood I make a vow. As long as there is breath in my lungs and strength in my body I'm going to protect anyone who puts their faith in me, young or old, sick or healthy, friend or stranger. I will protect them with all I have, until my dying breath. And if I am to fail I shall pay the penalty of the blood upon which I make this vow."

He released his hand and stood in the water for a little longer, blood still dripping from his fingertips.

When he was a child his mother told him many stories of great heroes who made dramatic vows and those stories always stuck with him, he remembered one story in particular where the hero named Hashara actually lost the final battle with the villain. To fix his mistake and save the day he ended up sacrificing himself for the good of everyone else. Jariko thought this was a very odd story because in almost every other story the heroes got a happy ending. He remembered he liked this story because after the hero lost, he vowed to never lose again and promised no one else would die as long as he fought and in the final battle. He stuck to his vow and died protecting it and everyone else. Thinking about this story comforted Jariko. He thought he might not be a hero now but if he stuck to his vow, one day he might be. He then turned around and walked back over to the fire, tearing a piece of cloth from his shirt and wrapping his hand, then laid back down. He stared up at the stars for several hours, silent as a mouse and still as a tree until the sun crept out from the horizon behind him. A new day had dawned, and like a phoenix reborn in the ashes of the previous day, the sun rose anew, shining brighter than before.

Chapter Eleven: New Journey

The sun crept over the horizon and Jariko stayed motionless as everyone awoke and started to stretch, walking over to the water's edge to wash and drink. Irabella and Mutanna woke up and began to discuss what they would do next.

"We need to leave as soon as possible otherwise we will miss registration!" Irabella insisted as she stood up and brushed the sand off of her legs.

"I agree, but we are taking Jariko with us." Mutana said.

"What?! Why?" Irabella shouted as her eyes darted over to Jariko, making sure he was still asleep.

"Because we both owe him our lives and there's something about him that I like." Mutana replied, stretching and cracking her neck. "Besides, I can tell you like him," Mutana said, winking. Irabella turned and blushed. Irabella then pointed her hand to the pile of burnt wood and a large, charred log began floating into the air.

"Say that again!" Irabella said threateningly, but Mutana just laughed and walked over to Jariko, dropped to her knees and shook him gently.

"Jariko? Everyone's waking up, we need to go," she said softly.

He opened his eyes and pretended to wake up.

"Oh, good morning," Jariko said, trying to stretch but forgetting about his injuries and recoiling in pain.

"Are you sure you don't want me to look at your wounds? I might be able to help," Mutana said.

"No, no, I'll be fine," Jariko said. "I just need to rest. I've always healed fast." Jariko smiled at Mutana as he said this and struggled to his feet. As he did, the rest of the survivors on the beach all walked over to Jariko and overwhelmed him with gratitude. Now the shock had worn off for most of them they could appreciate what he had done for them. He had never been so embarrassed and excited to get so much attention from so many beautiful women. After each of them had given their thanks to Jariko they left and headed back west to see if there were any survivors left in Rybalin.

"They will be fine," Mutana explained. "Orkestra will be sending aid any day now."

This comforted Jariko and he waved them goodbye, however the two women were still in shock from what had happened and they didn't seem interested in moving so the others had to pick them up and guide them home.

I hope they get better, Jariko thought trying to hide the guilt he felt. Suddenly, Bombo came up from behind Jariko and as gently as an Ogre can, pushed him.

"Jabo, we leave too," Bombo said. "We head back to mountain and make home." Bombo couldn't contain his excitement at this prospect and grabbed Jariko and hugged him, Jariko flinched from the pain of his injury but the hug was still welcome.

"Thanks, Jabo. We giants friends," Bombo exclaimed as he beat his chest, Jariko returned the gesture and the Ogres all slowly started to walk down the beach heading north. Jariko hoped he would get to see Bombo again. He had no idea how he would ever find him, but maybe someday.

Jariko turned to face Irabella and smiled. She rolled her eyes, crossed her arms and started to walk in the opposite direction.

"Where's she going?" Jariko asked.

"South - we are going to Orkestra, remember? You're coming too," Mutana said, smiling.

Jariko still hadn't decided what he was going to do, if he left he might never go home thus truly abandoning his mother's memory. On the other hand, old man Rolo and his wife were going to be staying there so they would keep it safe until the day Jariko could go home. He stood there in silence with a worried look on his face for a few moments before Mutana spoke.

"Look, all I ask is you escort us to Orkestra and cheer me on in the tournament. I will personally walk you home if that's what you want to do."

Jariko considered this for a moment.

"Okay," Jariko replied grinning uncontrollably, "But I need to send word to Rolo as soon as possible. He's probably worried sick by now."

Jariko rubbed the back of his neck. He was feeling guilty that Rolo was probably at his house with no idea what had happened to the town or him. He quickly forgot his guilt, however, as Mutana turned around gleefully and started to walk after Irabella. Jariko chased after both of them breaking into a jog.

"How far is it to Orkestra?" Jariko asked, panting heavily.

"Around three days if we don't make any long stops along the way. The tournament starts in five days so we should have enough time to get there and settle in before it starts," Mutana said.

"What about supplies? We don't have any food and I haven't eaten for a whole day." Jariko asked as his stomach rumbled like an angry buffalo.

"There's a small fishing village half a day's walk from here. We should be able to quickly get some supplies together and carry on," Mutana explained putting her hand on Jariko's shoulder. It was gentle but still hurt from his wounds.

"I'm glad you're coming with us, we owe you, our lives." She looked at him and for the first time she looked serious. Jariko nodded and smiled. The guilt of the people that died in the escape still hung over him like a rain cloud, but he didn't want to think about it. He distracted himself by thinking about everything he wanted to do in Orkestra. Jariko had always wanted to see the King's palace and also see the great hall of the city's chapel: the Cosilica. They say Agorith built the chapel himself - the original artwork still decorates the room; fifty feet high and glass windows stretch from the floor to the ceiling. Jariko had never been one for art, but the stories of the chapel made it sound so magnificent that even he could appreciate the craftsmanship.

They had been walking for roughly an hour on the damp, loose sand and stone before they finally saw Irabella standing on the top of a mound of large rocks looking out into the distance. There was a steep sandy hill leading off the beach and Jariko struggled to keep his footing as they made the climb. Mutana slipped a couple of times before they both had made it to the top of the beach and Irabella was now sitting on the rocks waiting for them.

"I can see a town about two miles that way," Irabella said, pointing.

Mutana nodded, still out of breath from the climb, and all three started walking together once again.

The walk was peaceful for a time as they made their way through the fields. The land was scattered with patches of trees and bushes over the vast uneven countryside. There wasn't really a path, but the grass had been crushed and made muddy by what looked like tracks from a wagon sneaking through the terrain. They followed the track for an hour and the land seemed rather empty. Then the strain of his sleepless night started to take effect on Jariko. His eyes became too heavy to keep open and he found himself stumbling and struggling to walk straight. He reached into his bag and pulled out his bottle of medicine, he took two gulps of the liquid before he put it safely back into his bag.

"What is that stuff?" Irabella asked, "I saw some empty bottles of it at your house."

Jariko blushed and hesitated to answer.

"Ever since I was a kid I've always had trouble staying awake at times. I would fall asleep in the most inconvenient places and this medicine helps to keep me awake. Old man Rolo made it for me," Jariko finally answered, embarrassed at such a strange problem.

"So, what's in it?" Irabella asked.

"I'm not really sure, but it tastes really good. Wanna try?" Jariko said, pulling the bottle back out and handing it to her. Irabella hesitated and smelt the bottle, then put it to her lips and tried the medicine. She was pleasantly surprised and took another drink.

"I wouldn't take too much," Jariko said.

"It tastes sweet!" Irabella said, "I think it's just some kind of sugar and water." She said, handing him the bottle back.

"Oh, that must be why I like it so much," Jariko replied, making Irabella laugh.

"You're way too trusting to drink a potion like that and not even know what's in it," Irabella said, still giggling. Jariko thought this was ironic since she had just done the same thing but just shrugged and put the bottle back into his bag.

After their chat Irabella seemed strangely happy and was walking faster than Jariko and Mutana. She seemed determined to get to the town in record time.

"Come on! I can see the town!" Irabella shouted from the bottom of a hill. Jariko and Mutana made their way down and after passing a few trees and muddy puddles, the image of the town became clear as they saw a dozen wooden cabins just like Jariko's house with trees growing in between them.

A cobbled road had appeared under their feet as they entered the town, uneven due to the hundreds of stones of all shapes and sizes that had been embedded into the ground, making it hard to get a good footing as they walked through the old town. They noticed a small market was set up along the road as they entered. A handful of people browsed the stands. They sold mostly fish and bread and household goods, however, Mutana noticed a strange sign hanging in one of the alleyways saying:

Bagnar's collection of goods and bads this way

"Perfect!" Mutana shouted as she walked in between two market stalls and down the short alleyway and through the open door to the shop. Irabella was still looking at the stalls and trying to decide what she wanted to eat, so Jariko followed Mutana down the alley into the shop. A loud and deep voice boomed across the room as Jariko entered.

"Welcome! I'm Bagnar and these are my goods and bads!" The glorious voice came from the corner of the room drawing Jariko's attention. As he made his way through the cluttered room he couldn't help but be amazed by the piles of knickknacks and collectables piled high to the ceiling, covering every shelf, and there were chests spilling over with all kinds of strange objects. Mutana was crouching on the floor looking through one of the chests filled with what looked like magical items.

Jariko approached the man behind the counter and to his amazement it was an Orcmul, or Orc for short. Jariko had never seen an Orc before due to their rarity in Concorvia and their tendency to travel. This made it all the stranger. He had never heard of an Orc with a shop before or at least one not on wheels.

The Orc was short with reddish brown skin and a large belly flopping over his belt like the top of a muffin spilling out of the ill fitted top and waistcoat. He had pitch black hair but only on the side of his head. An unfortunate bald spot had stripped the top of his head. His two-pointed ears flopped down and two large sharp teeth stuck up out of his mouth.

In his deep voice and strange accent, Bagnar spoke again: "'Ello young man, 'ow can I help ya today?" Bagnar asked with a smile that seemed too happy to be real.

"Oh, I don't have any money, I'm just looking around." Jariko said.

"Don't worry about that, whatever he gets I'll pay for it when I'm done!" Mutana shouted from the other side of the room. She was still looking through the chest of broken staffs and empty bottles and lots of strange magic components.

"Well, in that case, what can I do for you?" Bagnar asked again, still uncomfortably smiling.

"Well... a bed roll? And maybe a map?" Jariko replied, trying not to ask for too much, not wanting to take advantage of Mutana's generosity.

"Ah, the essentials for a wanderer. Aye, not a problem at all young man, right this way."

He shuffled over to an old bookcase. It had so many books that they had been stuffed in every crack and balancing on every flat surface. He looked intently at the bookshelf for a minute.

"Ah, 'ere you go." Bagnar leant over and pulled out an old, folded piece of paper from the bottom shelf. He unfolded it and shook it and a cloud of dust that had accumulated on the piece of paper exploded out into the room.

"There you go, it might be a bit outdated, but it has the basics for traveling Concorvia. Now for the bed roll..." Bagnar shuffled off again. He stopped and looked up at the ceiling and there, pinned to the roof was a net holding a dozen bedrolls, Bagnar pulled on the net and pulled one out.

"There you go my friend, a map and a bedroll. I'll charge your pretty friend when she's ready but for now is there anything else you need?" Bagnar obviously wanted to get as much money as he could, but before Jariko could answer Mutana shouted again.

"You need a weapon, Jariko! Some cold steel would have been handy yesterday!" She turned and looked at Jariko, smiled and winked before turning back. Jariko didn't know what to say, he felt guilty for taking Mutana's money, but it must've been her way of thanking him.

"Well, I keep all the weapons around the back for safe keepin'," Bagnar explained. "Follow me!" Bagnar shuffled through a door into the back room and Jariko followed.

The back room was worse than the front, full of mountains of random assortments and junk. Jariko could barely move without knocking something over or nearly tripping. He found Bagnar by the back door standing next to a chest overflowing with weapons and tools.

"Take your pick!" Bagnar exclaimed, stretching his arm out. Jariko had never even held a weapon let alone used one, how could he know which one he should choose?

The chest was filled with every kind of weapon you could think of. There were axes, swords, spears, knives, bows, a few pistols and even some weapons Jariko didn't know the name of, but he could tell how to use them just by looking at them. He liked to fight up close, so he didn't want a bow and arrow, he didn't want something that took too much skill like a sword or a knife, he just wanted something simple and easy to use.

He kept rummaging through, then in the corner of his eye, he saw an axe leant up against the wall separate from the other weapons.

"What about that?" Jariko asked, walking over to examine the axe. It was a long-bearded axe that resembled an executioner's axe, but the metal was thicker and curved right back to the light brown wooden handle it sat on. The handle was too short to be used as a two-handed axe, but it had a leather strap wrapped around the handle for grip. There were also strange engravings and drawings decorating the steel, but Jariko didn't recognize any of them.

"You don't want that, kid - it's too heavy to be a one-handed axe and the handle is too short for a two-handed axe. I just use it to chop wood," Bagnar explained.

Jariko picked up the axe but it didn't seem too heavy for him and felt comfortable to swing with one hand, he didn't know what it was but he wanted the axe.

"So, you won't sell it?" Jariko asked.

"Kid, everythin' is for sale 'ere if you want it that bad," Bagnar chuckled. Jariko nodded in approval grinning like a child and the two walked back to the front of the shop. Mutana had finally finished rummaging and was waiting at the till with a basket of goodies that she had found.

"An axe? Yeah, that seems about right," Mutana said, smiling.

“That'll be one 'undred gold pieces.” Bagnar said after looking through Mutana's basket and adding it onto what Jariko already had.

“How about fifty?” Mutana asked, not breaking eye contact. Jariko could tell she was used to haggling.

“Yeah, alright then,” Bagnar replied reluctantly.

“But only cause you're the prettiest face I've seen in awhile,” Bagnar said flirtatiously, smiling at Mutana.

“You're too kind,” Mutana said awkwardly, smiling and picking up her things before leaving. Jariko followed waving goodbye to Bagnar.

"You two are welcome back any time." Bagnar while waving back as they left.

“Now, where did Irabella go?” Mutana said to herself as they wandered back to the market.

Chapter Twelve: Unwanted Attention

Jariko and Mutana walked back through the alleyway and over to the market. Looking around they couldn't find Irabella anywhere, and so they walked over to the fish stall where she was standing when they left. Jariko jumped up and down trying to get a good look around to spot her, but nothing. They made their way through the small crowd of people, but Irabella was nowhere to be seen. Mutana became anxious, panicking as she frantically walked around. Once she reached the end of the market, she was extremely worried, then she began to call Irabella's name.

"Irabella!" Mutana called, "Bella!" She called again, but there was no response. Jariko began to panic and started to call for her as well.

"Irabella!" He shouted, "Irabella!" But still nothing.

They had no idea where she could have gone - the town was small enough to see all the way to the other side.

They decided to split up and try and check all of the buildings in town, but most of them were homes so there was no reason Irabella would be in one. Just as Jariko was making his way around the corner of a large wooden building, he heard a young woman's scream: it was Irabella. He ran around the corner just in time to see a wagon with four men. Two of them were lifting Irabella into the back of the wagon while the other two were getting the horses ready, they then climbed into the seats at the front of the wagon.

"HEY!" Jariko shouted as he charged towards the men. The two men at the front of the wagon spun their heads around, the sight of Jariko charging scared the pair and they whipped the reins and the horses began to run. The pair of men holding Irabella leaped into the back of the wagon just in time. Jariko couldn't let them get away but suddenly he realised he was still holding his brand new axe in his hand and with one mighty swing he threw his axe at the wagon with so much force that when the axe hit the entire back half exploded into shards of wood and splinters, tearing one of the back wheels off and causing the wagon to hit the ground and become stuck.

The pair of men at the front jumped off the wagon and pulled out their swords while running to meet Jariko head on. Suddenly, a large ball of raging fire came into Jariko's vision almost blinding him and incinerating the two men where they stood, leaving only their swords and a pile of blackened ash. Jariko turned around and saw Mutana standing twenty feet away with her hand stuck out, still smoking. Her face was one of pure rage, like a mother protecting her child. She walked over to the wagon with Jariko in tow and with no hesitation pulled out a dagger from her belt and lifted it into the air but when opening the sheet covering the back of the stranded wagon she saw that the men were already dead, or at the very least unconscious, and standing over them was Irabella, brushing the dust and mud off her robes. Without hesitation Mutana grabbed Irabella and pulled her into a hug. The two stood there for a moment until Irabella noticed Jariko and pulled herself away.

“Did they hurt you!?” Mutana asked frantically, holding Irabella.

“I’m fine, these wimps hit like old ladies,” she said, kicking the unconscious men.

“Why were they after you?” Jariko asked.

“I don't know, they didn't have time to introduce themselves,” she replied, sarcasm seeping out of her mouth.

“Hey! We just saved you, the least you could do is be grateful!” Jariko stated slightly irritated by her tone.

“I didn't need saving, thank you very much. I was just going to be a little more subtle about my escape than blowing up a wagon and killing two of them. How did you do that by the way, how strong are you?” Irabella said, seeming to get suspicious of Jariko. He looked away uncomfortably not wanting to answer and changed the subject.

“Maybe these two guys can tell us what they wanted when they wake up?” He said with a slight tremble in his voice.

“Good idea,” Mutana said, composing herself.

She dragged one out and propped him up against a boulder next to the wagon. She then pulled a container of water out of her bag, poured some on his head and the man woke up in a panic and screamed.

“Hey!” Mutana shouted, slapping the man to calm him down. “What did you want with Irabella?!”

The man's eyes darted in between the three of them not taking any notice of the question. He suddenly tried to climb to his feet and run, but Irabella raised her hand and pinned him against the boulder.

“What do you want with me?!” She asked.

“I... I don't know... some guy paid us and said there would be a witch in this town, and we needed to take her to him.” His voice was frantic and full of fear.

“We didn't know who the witch was or why he wanted her, but he paid us a lot of gold to do it and when we saw your robes, we knew you were a witch.” He seemed to be telling the truth, but this didn't calm Irabella down at all.

“I'm a sorceress, so don't call me a witch. Now who paid you!?” She shouted, tightening her grip around his throat.

"I... I don't... I don't know... He only spoke to my boss, the guy driving the wagon!" The man shouted gasping for air. Mutana looked over to the piles of ash that had been the men driving the wagon.

"Shit!" Mutana said, standing up and walking back over to the wagon. Irabella released the man and walked off in the opposite direction, too angry to talk anymore. Coughing and trying to catch his breath the man stood up.

"Look, I'm sorry, I was just trying to make some money, we were never gunna hurt anyone." The man tried to explain to Jariko, but before Jariko responded, Mutana walked back over.

"Do you know anything about this guy? What he looked like or why he paid you so much?" The man shook his head.

"I never met him and the only thing my boss ever said about him was that he was creepy but rich and he met him in Orkestra. I swear I don't know anything else." He appeared to be telling the truth, so Mutana let the man go. He walked over to the wagon and picked up his still unconscious friend.

"I am truly sorry," he said, then turned and walked into the town with his friend on his shoulder. A small crowd had gathered after hearing all the shouting and noises. The three of them watched him until he was out of site.

Mutana turned to Jariko, "If there's someone in Orkestra that would go to these lengths to find a sorceress, then we need to start watching our backs from now on." She looked around seeing all the attention they were getting, "And we should really leave." Jariko nodded and after a few minutes to compose themselves they left the town, not wanting any more unwanted attention. The three of them continued their journey before any more trouble found them.

They walked for miles down a dirt track passing other adventurers and merchants along the way, making sure to watch their back every time someone passed them. They were all on edge and expecting to be attacked again, but after hours of walking it was rather uneventful. The sun began to set, turning the sky into a fiery red and orange once again.

"We should find somewhere to sleep for the night." Mutana said looking around the area. She then spotted a rocky structure composed of large boulders and a small cave just large enough for the three to settle down for the night. Jariko began collecting sticks to build a fire but Mutana interrupted him.

"No fires, we are safer under the cover of night."

She smiled and walked back over to the cave. It wasn't cold so Jariko didn't mind, but when he walked over to the cave Irabella was shivering, curled up in the corner clutching her arms. Jariko removed the bedroll he had bought in the town and passed it to her, he knew she must have been exhausted because she didn't say anything mean or pretend, she wasn't cold, she simply smiled and accepted the kind gesture.

Jariko sat down on the floor and tried to get comfortable. He found a nice pillow shaped rock and leaned against it.

Just as Jariko started to drift off, Mutana spoke.

"Anyone want me to hear a story?"

Irabella stayed silent and as much as Jariko wanted to sleep, the thought of being told a story like his mother used to was too much for him to resist.

"Do you know the one about the War of Creation?" Jariko asked softly.

"Jariko, I'm a sorceress from the church of Primak. Of course I do!" Mutana chuckled. "Where should I start... ah, I know. After summoning all the Creators to Primak, Tando issued a challenge to create two of the most perfect creatures they could imagine. The other Creators scoffed at this challenge, but they had no choice for Tando had promised to lend them some of his overwhelming power and with it they could be whole once again.

After accepting the challenge, each Creator left to work on their creations, however, Primak stayed. He simply raised his hand and a spiral of dirt and water began to rise up from the ground coming together to form a skeleton, organs and then a complete human male body. He raised his other hand and the same magical act happened but this time a human female body. Tando asked Primak why he had made his creature look the same as the Creators but so weak and fragile, he simply responded: 'Because they are us, but better.'

Tando didn't understand this and in his anger was inspired to make his creature. He raised his hands and before him formed a creature with anger and malice in its eyes, he purposely made it resemble the human Primak had created, but twice the size and with four arms, each pulsating with pure strength and destruction. He wanted to show Primak what true perfection looked like, and so the Giants were formed, a living insult in the face of Primak.

Meanwhile, Sacula, a being of patience, was wandering through a thick jungle teeming with life. She noticed a strange creature hanging from a tree. It moved so slowly that those very trees had begun to grow upon it. A sloth with white and green fur, three long claws on each hand and a sweet looking face, then at her feet she felt something walking along the grass. She thought it was a rock but when she leaned in to get a closer look she realised it was a sweet little creature as well, moving just as slow as the sloth but with a large shell on its back for protection. These creatures impressed Sacula so much she had decided what her creations would look like and headed back to the others.

Termatil was a being of stealth and cunning and found himself wandering through some woods, each step crunching on leaves and the wind whistling through the trees. He stopped when he heard something else making its way through the forest. He saw a small rabbit gathering and eating berries. He stopped to admire the rabbit until suddenly an orange furred fox darted out of the bushes and clamped its teeth around the rabbit’s neck. Termatil was impressed with this creature's stealth and speed. He continued watching the fox eat the rabbit for a few more moments before another creature appeared but this time descending from the trees. A small monkey swung down from a branch above the fox and grabbed the berries that the rabbit had been eating without the fox ever noticing. Termatil chuckled and left the woods smiling and returned to the others knowing what his creations would look like.

Once Termatil and Sacula returned they saw Primak and Tando's creations standing by their masters and in the corner of their eyes they saw Quarbela was beginning to create her own creatures. She had always been a very jealous being and always hated Primak, so after a few moments her creations were complete. One with fair skin and long golden hair and deep blue eyes. It resembled Primak's humans but with long pointed ears, obviously her way to show that she could make a more beautiful creation than Primak, and she named them the Elchrit or Elf. Her other creation was the complete opposite, as a form of insult to the humans Primak had created much like the Giants. Her next creation had sickly green skin and pitch-black hair and its ears were pointed but drooping down. She had created the Gormens or Goblins.

Quintala was a being of love and peace and didn't want to take part in Tando's challenge. She wandered the landscape for many miles and was amazed at the beauty of the scenery. She saw many strange and interesting creatures along her way and fell in love with every single one. After a while she found herself at a riverbank. She knelt and put her hand in the water. The cool rushing water felt relaxing, running through her fingers and she began to play with the water giggling as she did so until she heard a noise next to her. She looked and saw a magnificent stag drinking from the river. The sight of this creature took her breath away and she couldn't look away. Once the stag had finished its drink, it looked up and stared back at her. After a few moments she realised it was not looking at her but the small bird that had perched itself on her shoulder without her knowing. She raised her hand and the little bird jumped onto her finger and sang a song. Quintala smiled and slowly moved her hand over to the stag and the bird then jumped and perched itself on the antlers of the stag. The two creatures then left peacefully and Quintala watched them, a single tear running down her face. She didn't know why she was crying but, in that moment, she realised that all of this life needed to be protected. She returned to the other Creators with her creations.

Last to return was Saxunda. He was a being of ferocity and anger. He had found himself at the edge of a great sea. He stood staring out at the open ocean entranced by its untameable nature. He was furious that Tando had betrayed him, and it filled him with rage, looking upon these unending crashing waves and the ferocity of the sea almost as if he was looking at himself, gave him a sense of tranquillity that he had never felt before.

The ocean was like an old friend he had not seen in a long time, and it understood his pain and anger. At this time of meditation, he noticed in the distance large birds diving into the water to catch fish. He kept his eye on one particular bird, watching it fly in circles in the sky and just as it dove into the sea a hurling mass lunged out of the water, grabbing the bird mid-flight. This huge shark began to tear the bird apart in the water turning it red before swimming away, leaving the pieces of the floating carcass in the water. A few moments later from behind him, an alligator made its way to the water after hearing the noises. It sunk under the water silently before exploding from below, tearing the last pieces of flesh the shark had left before making its way back to the beach. Seeing this transpire Saxunda was reminded of his own blood lust and this gave him the motivation to return to win Tando's challenge with his own Creations.

This next part of the story is my favourite..."

Mutana sat up and realised that Jariko and Irabella were already asleep. She smiled and laid back down.

"We can finish it tomorrow," she said. Closing her eyes, she began to plan what the next step of their journey would entail.

Chapter Thirteen: Arrival

It had been two days since they left the small village. The journey so far had been pleasantly uneventful. Irabella was still on edge, looking over her shoulder to check if Jariko and Mutana were still in her sight whenever she led the group. They had taken turns leading - Jariko followed the map he had bought but Mutana and Irabella preferred to wing it. They mostly followed the road, but Mutana tried a few shortcuts that turned out not to be shorter at all, sometimes leading them in circles. She pretended she did it on purpose, but Jariko could tell she was lost and quickly found the way back to the road mostly using skills his mother taught him and a little luck. Once the sun was high in the sky, they knew they only had a few hours of sunlight left, they needed to get to Orkestra by the end of tomorrow if Mutana was going to make it in time for the tournament.

They walked tirelessly until Jariko stopped. He could smell something that was familiar to him.

"You okay?" Mutana asked. Jariko looked at her in horror as he realised what he could smell. He broke out into a sprint down the road and Mutana and Irabella gave chase. They tried to keep up with him, but Jariko was too fast. They had lost sight of him but kept running, and after a few minutes they caught up to him and stopped, panting heavily trying to catch their breath.

"Why are you running?!" Irabella asked, annoyed as she approached him, but then she realised Jariko was standing on the edge of a rocky cliff and in front of them was the heart-breaking realisation that they were truly off course: all they could see was the unending deep blue of the ocean.

“What?! I don't understand - we should've arrived at Orkestra before getting to the coastline,” Irabella said, confused. Jariko looked at his map and tried to figure out where they were.

“Why didn't the road take us to Orkestra?” Mutana asked, frustrated, and exhausted.

“It would have but it looks like we missed the crossroad, we are on the south coast.” explained Jariko pointing at the map.

“We’re gonna miss registration,” Irabella announced, defeated while laying down on the floor.

“Do we have time to turn back and find the crossroad?”

“It's at least a day's walk from here. We would be better off following the coast until we find this little village here,” Jariko said pointing to the village on his map.

“From there we might be able to buy a horse and just make it in time.”

This plan lifted Mutana’s spirit.

“Well, come on then, let's hurry!” Mutana exclaimed but Irabella wasn't convinced, the last few days had been too much for her and Jariko could tell she wouldn't make it to Orkestra. Mutana was already walking west, following the coastline and Irabella stumbled to her feet. Jariko wanted to help but he didn’t know how. Then he got an idea - he ran in front of Irabella and fell to one knee.

“What are you doing, weirdo!” She asked.

“We both know you have nothing left and at this rate we won't make it, so climb on.”

“You have to be kidding,” she said, crossing her arms.

"Do you want to get to the tournament in time?!" Jariko said. She paused for a moment before dropping her arms in a resentful agreement and climbed onto Jariko's back. Mutana was already almost out of sight, so Jariko started running to catch up to her.

"Am I not heavy?" Irabella asked.

"No, not really. Just be careful my axe doesn't cut you!"

The next few hours Irabella was strangely kind to Jariko, not like her normal self. She had begun to warm up to him and after all he had done, she began to trust him. Only Mutana had had this privilege before him. Along the way Irabella and Jariko opened up to each other, telling stories about their lives and what they wanted to do.

"I want to be a famous sorceress one day, but Mutana has a lot more to teach me before then."

"But you're so good with your magic, what more can there be to learn?" Jariko asked genuinely interested in the topic.

"Are you kidding? Yes, I'm good at magic but that is only the first step. I also need a good understanding of the planets and stars and their part in the universe. People can study for years and still end up barely scratching the surface to understand how the universe works."

"So, by planets you mean the other Creators?" Jariko asked.

"Yes, exactly! The other five planets in our solar system are where each of the other Creators live. Sacula,

Termatil, Quarbela, Saxunda, my favourite Quintala and of course Primak all gravitate around Tando which is our sun. That's why most mages are priests, because you can't begin to understand the magic without understanding the Creators that brought us into being, and you can't appreciate the Creators without understanding the universe they created. That's why we all study astrology and science as well as the teaching of the Creators."

"What happens when you understand all three of those things and know how to use all five classes of magic?" Jariko asked. Mutana interrupted, evidently listening to their conversation the whole time.

"Pure Magic, an unrestrained version of all the other five classes. The five classes are just the five different ways you can use magic, split up for easier understanding and training, however, once someone unlocks Pure Magic they can combine them all to do basically anything, only limited by the amount of magic the wielder has at their disposal. Theoretically, you could create life. That is the power of the Creators."

"Has anyone ever gotten that kind of power?" Jariko asked in shock that such power was even real.

"Yes, but only two. Agorith the first mage and founder to the Church of Primak. He was the one who discovered all the ways you can use magic and separated them into their classes."

"And the second man?"

"His apprentice, although I don't remember his name. There are rumours that some have unlocked Pure Magic up in Deuterra, but I don't believe it."

Just as Mutana finished what she was saying, Irabella gasped in excitement.

"Look! Smoke rising!" She pointed at the smoke peeking out from behind some trees.

"That must be the village!" Jariko exclaimed, breaking out into a jog with Irabella still clinging onto his back. Mutana started running as well to keep up with them. They reached the tree line and kept going, not stopping to take care through the trees. Then, as if being greeted by Primak himself, the small village was a divine sight to behold.

"We made it!" Jariko shouted, unable to contain his excitement and relief.

"Just in time as well, the sun is starting to set," Irabella said, looking up to the sky.

The three weary travellers approached the village and sitting on a stool on the outskirts was an old man holding a stick. In a croaky voice the old man stopped them.

"What do you want?!" He was holding his stick up to block the road.

"We are on our way to Orkestra," Jariko answered, not wanting to offend the man.

"You've missed it boy," he said scowling at Jariko.

"We missed the road and we were hoping to stay here for the night and head there in the morning," Mutana interjected. Having not noticed the two sorceresses, the old man stood up in respect once he realised he was speaking to a priest of Primak.

"Oh, I'm so sorry ma'am. There's the Drunken Macaroo straight down the road there," he said lifting his stick to point.

"Thank you, you're a gentleman," Mutana said, smiling. The old man smiled back, blushing as he sat back down. They continued walking down the road and Jariko turned to Mutana.

"What was that about?"

"People tend to show a lot of respect to priests and mages. Some mages can become well-known if they are good enough, that's why this tournament is such a big deal. It's a chance for civilians to see new mages that show a lot of promise, a chance to show off their powers and strengths. This gives the civilians the chance to see how powerful the church is and this helps them trust us in times of crisis."

"So, you're kinda famous?" Jariko asked.

"In Concorvia, yes. But not so much in other countries."

This excited Jariko - he had never felt so important before. He suddenly had a sense of honour as he embarked on this journey.

They got to the bottom of the road and saw the wooden sign hanging over the door: *The Drunken Macaroo.* The sign depicted a tankard pouring a liquid into the mouth of a Macaroo, a funny little creature resembling a monkey found in the north. They walked up the wooden steps and entered the inn. They were greeted by a gangly Goblin.

"Welcome, welcome. Come in from the cold and warm up by the fire." He waved his hand in the direction of the fireplace in the middle of the room. It was surrounded by wooden tables and chairs, but the rest of the room was fairly empty with large beams supporting the upstairs and candles on the walls. Jariko put Irabella down and they took a seat by the fire while Mutana paid for the rooms.

"Thank you Jariko," Irabella said faintly while sticking her hands out towards the fire. Jariko didn't respond, he just gave her a smile. Ten minutes had passed and Mutana returned.

"I got two rooms, Irabella and I will share and Jariko you can have the room on the right as you go up the stairs."

"Thank you," he replied gratefully. He picked his bag up from the floor and they made their way upstairs.

"Good night," Mutana called as they walked past Jariko's room as he closed the door.

"Good night," he replied. He turned around and as if he had died, he fell face first onto the bed, and within seconds was asleep.

The sun rose on a new morning and Jariko slowly woke up. He sat on the bed realising he had slept in. He panicked for a moment, quickly reaching to grab his bag when he heard a knock at the door.

“Come in,” he called and Irabella walked into his room.

“Did you sleep in that dirty poncho? I've never seen you take it off!” Irabella said, turning up her nose to him.

“My mother told me to never take it off while I was away from home,” he replied smiling awkwardly and picking up his bag and axe.

“I'm sure she didn't mean literally, but whatever floats your boat.”

They walked out the room together and headed down the stairs to Mutana sitting by the fireplace.

“Good morning,” Mutana said cheerfully, “I spoke to the innkeeper and he said there is a stable on the west side of town. We should be able to buy some horses there."

She stood up and led the way out of the inn. Jariko suddenly realised that Runner was still out there somewhere. He hadn't seen him since Rybalin. He was confident he probably just went home. He needed to remind himself to ask old man Rolo when he wrote his letter home.

The three left the inn and began to make their way to the west side of town. The streets were busier than they were last night but only a few dozen people were walking around. Jariko began to daydream as he had found himself doing a lot on this journey before suddenly hearing some shouting. Everyone turned to look up the road to see what the noise was. It was a young Marvub boy, the rare monkey race from the country of Domadon. He came running out of an alleyway, followed by a tall Goblin no older than Jariko.

“Help, they stole my gold!” The Goblin shouted as he ran down the road trying to chase the young Marvub. He ran straight past Mutana and Irabella who were ahead but paid no attention to the Marvub only watching the Goblin as he ran towards them. Jariko was able to grab his arm and stop him in his tracks. The Marvub boy looked up at Jariko in terror as the Goblin caught up.

“Thank you, I had completely lost sight of him,” he said panting heavily. “The little bastard used perception magic to go invisible and steal my purse,” he kneeled down to look the boy in the eye.

“But I guess you couldn't hold it for long could ya, rookie,” he smiled as he said this but the young Marvub boy was still too scared to talk.

Mutana came over to try and diffuse the situation.

“Good catch Jariko. I didn't even see him run past,” she leant down smiling. “Hey kid, why don't you give this young man his money back,” she said. He nodded and with a shaking hand the boy returned the purse to the Goblin and Jariko let him go. He shot off at speed quickly disappearing into the crowd.

“Hey why’d you let him go! I was gonna… hey you guys are mages too!?” The Goblin said in disbelief looking at Mutana and Irabella. “Guess me and my brother aren't the only ones to get lost,” he said, laughing. “I’m Kellarom and that ugly guy running over to us is my brother Moritus." He pointed as he said it and they saw another young Goblin running towards them. He looked older than Kellarom. It was obvious they were brothers, both tall with green skin, long drooping ears and short black spiky hair, but Moritus had a black beard covering half his face.

"You idiot - how could you let that kid steal from you? And a novice Class One user no less. I thought I taught you better than that," Moritus said, scolding Kellarom. While they were arguing Jariko noticed they were wearing white robes like Mutana and Irabella although shorter with their sleeves rolled up as well as black trousers.

"You guys are mages too?" Jariko announced interrupting their squabble.

"Oh, yes, sorry, where are my manners?" Moritus said, bowing in respect. "We are priests of Primak and we come from Valabur in the east. We thought we had found a quick way to Orkestra but ended up missing it entirely," he said with embarrassment.

"Don't be embarrassed - we did the same thing," Mutana said, holding out her hand. Moritus shook it and laughed softly. "We were just about to go to the stables to get some horses. We should make it in time for registration on horseback. I assume that's why you're heading to Orkestra?" Mutana asked.

"Yes, of course, I should've guessed you would be taking part in the tournament as well. If you don't mind, my brother and I would be honoured to join you on the last part of your trip," Moritus answered, smiling.

Mutana returned the smile blushing - the two Goblins subtly flirting. Then the small group all headed to the stables together. They found it with almost no trouble and proceeded to buy four horses. To save money, it was decided that Mutana and Irabella would share while Jariko, Kellarom and Moritus all had their own. They set off northwest from the town straight for Orkestra. Mutana, Irabella and Moritus were ahead while Jariko and Kellarom were in the back talking about their adventures over the last few days. Jariko told Kellarom all about the Roach-lin den and Rybalin and Kellarom was awestruck.

"I can't believe you guys survived that! And befriending Ogres? I mean come on, that's crazy!"

Jariko nodded but talking about it was still upsetting for him. His eyes fell and he stared down at his lap.

"Not everyone survived. We lost a few people and Ogres in the escape," Jariko said, looking back on that day.

"Yeah, but you saved so many more, that's worth being proud of," Kellarom replied, sounding sincere. Jariko smiled but wanting to change the subject he asked Kellarom about himself and his brother.

"So, are you entering the tournament as well?" Jariko asked.

"No way, I'm still just a novice. My brother is the true badass - he's been teaching me since we were young. We are class three mages so we can summon Golems to fight for us. Don't think I can't fight - I can use this thing very well too," he said patting the wooden staff that was strapped to his back. "I can also use a little class five magic in the form of energy weapons, but not much more, I'm teaching myself..." he paused for a moment. "Someday I want to be as good as my brother, but right now I can only make basic Golems. Same sort of size as us and ethereal weapons, but my brother can make stone golems twenty feet tall, even ones without legs that he can stand inside and use as a shield."

"Could you show me some time?" Jariko asked giddy at the thought of seeing a stone golem.

"Yeah, sure! Come by when we are training in the city, I'll show you what I can do," Kellarom replied arrogantly smiling but Jariko could tell he didn't mean to sound cocky.

They talked for several more hours before they noticed the rest of their group stopped at the top of a hill. As they joined them they were stunned in disbelief as they looked ahead upon the countryside, but unlike the last few days this countryside wasn't empty. As far as they could see, there was life. A city so large none of them had seen anything like it before. They all stood speechless just wanting to take in the sight of the great capital city, Orkestra.

Chapter Fourteen: Orkestra

The sight of the great city was breath-taking. It was so much greater than the stories had depicted and so much more menacing. They continued walking towards the city and as it grew closer, growing in size every second, the true gravity of Jariko's adventure struck him. All he could think about was how proud his mother would be and how he wanted her there with him. She had always told him how she wanted to see the city so finally being here filled Jariko with an overwhelming feeling of happiness and triumph, but at the same time he felt distraught because even though she was there in mind, she wasn't there in body. No matter how much he pretended, deep down he knew she never got to see it and this was a harsh realisation for Jariko.

As they approached the city they could start to see the farms that peppered the land outside the city walls. The walls themselves were ten feet thick and thirty feet tall spanning the entire length of the city. There were five walls in total, each inside one another creating the layers of the city.

These walls split the city into sections or as they call them, districts. The first layer of the city was mainly houses, hundreds of homes were crammed into this district, giving it the name the Housing District but they were still the most valued and expensive homes to buy anywhere in the country.

The next was the Market District. As the name implies this was the main trading place for the city. Every kind of shop imaginable could be found in the Market District. It was the most sought-after location for any business or merchant to set up in and the gold was endlessly flowing through it.

The next district was the largest and took up most of the inner city. It was the Grand District and had a bit of everything, including small farms, mainly for the palace needs, as well as the army barracks, their training grounds and the famous Majuky colosseum, famous for the hundreds of thousands of people that travel from across the world to see fights, shows and many historical events. This was also where the upcoming tournament would be held.

Next was the Harmony District. Small and primarily for the church, the district held the main cathedral of Primak as well as a cemetery for the city and a handful of training schools for novice mages.

The innermost and smallest district but also the hardest to gain entry to was the Royal District which only had one thing inside its walls: the palace of the king. It is the home to the king of Concorvia and where the most esteemed and richest noblemen go to discuss politics, pass laws and is said to be so magnificent simply walking through the gates to this district can feel like stepping into another world.

Every district together made Orkestra, every layer making a semi-circle that had a twenty-mile circumference, sitting on the cliff edge of the coastline overlooking the sea. This makes the city the single most powerful and unchallenged in the entire world. Many had tried to burn and take the city but with the combined forces of the mages of the church and the king's royal army, only a few had ever landed on the shores of Concorvia. Due to the city being situated on the cliff edge, invaders had to come ashore further down the coastline, giving the guards time to intercept them before ever reaching the city, and thanks to the sheer size of the cliff that the city sits on, cannon fire is simply rendered useless. It is for these reasons Orkestra is known as the greatest power on Primak and the King is so well respected and feared by the other five Titans of the world.

The small group of adventurers approached the city gates still trying to take the sight in but overwhelmed by the size of the city. The walls were nothing but intimidating and the guards strategically placed along the top and the bottom of the wall made Jariko feel more than just a little uneasy.

They approached the stable a short walk from the main gate to tie their horses up when Jariko heard a loud crash and shouting coming from inside the small wooden house which the stables were a part of. A few moments later a man came bursting out of the door nearly taking it off its hinges and falling to the ground.

"Damn, blasted horse!" He said while climbing to his feet.

"There's a horse in there?" Irabella asked, more than a little confused.

"No normal horse that's for sure - found it eating all my hay half a week ago and it's been nothing but a nightmare ever since," the stableman said furiously. Jariko wasn't confused at all - there was only one horse in the world that fitted that description. After helping the man to his feet, he ran into the small house.

"Runner!" He exclaimed. "How did you get all the way here?" Jariko ran and gave Runner a huge hug.

"That's your horse?!" The man said angrily and more than a little surprised.

"Yes, I lost him a while ago during the attack on Rybalin. I'm so glad you're okay," Jariko exclaimed, hugging Runner again.

"You were at the attack on Rybalin?! The guards said no one had survived."

"Only us and a small group managed to make it out," Mutana interjected, sounding very professional to distract and change the subject. She continued. "We are mages from around Concorvia, here to enter the tournament. I was hoping you knew where we could go to register?"

"Well then, you better go speak to the guards at the main gate, they should know." The man pointed Mutana in the right direction before turning back to Jariko and raising a finger at him.

"Now, you, boy, you owe me for looking after your horse!"

"I'm going to be here for a few days, would you mind looking after him until my business is done?"

Jariko hugged Runner again and chased after the group before the man could reply.

"Bu..." The man tried to argue but didn't get the chance; Jariko had gone. He turned around just in time to see Runner start chewing on his bed sheet.

As they approached the main gate they were stopped by a guard. He was wearing a red tunic and black trousers tucked into his black books, a thick metal breastplate strapped to his torso and a helmet covering his head and face. All the guards were dressed the same, so they became indistinguishable from one another. The only noticeable difference was their weapon of choice. The guards at the main gate had large pole arms with a metal spike and curved blade at the top called billhooks or a bill.

"Halt! No one is allowed entry into the city without official business," the guard said with a stern and deep voice.

"We are here for the tournament. I am Mutana, representing Ferradon with my apprentice, Irabella."

Moritus then stepped forward.

"And I am Moritus representing Valabur with my apprentice Kellarom."

The guard glanced at their papers and waved them through the gate, however, Jariko was grabbed on the shoulder by the guard.

"What's your business boy?"

"He's with us," Mutana said. She stopped as the others carried on.

"Each mage is only allowed a single person to join them to help in any way." The guard pointed at Irabella. "You already have someone, now please move along."

Jariko's stomach sank. Had he come all this way just to be turned away at the gate? The thought did come to him to run inside, but he would be lucky if he didn't get caught immediately and killed. Mutana stayed to argue with the guard before another came to drag her through the gate. She began shouting and arguing. Then, Jariko had an idea.

"I have information on the attack at Rybalin," Jariko shouted so the guard would hear him over Mutana's yelling. They stopped for a moment before laughing.

"And what would a kid like you know about that, no one survived."

"It's true!" Mutana and Irabella shouted in unison. Amidst the shouting Jariko stuck his hand in his pocket and pulled out the large pincer he had ripped from the mouth of the king Roach-lin and the guards fell silent.

"Is that from a Roach-lin!?" One guard said.

"Not a normal one, look at the size of it," another guard replied in disbelief. They listened to Jariko as he explained what had happened and begrudgingly the guards let him through with the order to go and speak to their Commander. Jariko smiled and walked through the gate to the others. The feeling of relief was indescribable, however, he quickly forgot all about what had just happened when he took his first step into the great city. The feeling of relief was replaced with a feeling of amazement when he laid his eyes for the first time on the true city of Orkestra.

Jariko was in the Housing District of the city. The buildings were huge compared to his own, they were not made of wood but what looked like white rocks stacked on top of one another and large wooden beams supporting the structure along the edges as well as the window frames. The houses themselves were two stories high with thatched roofs, but due to the houses being so tightly packed, the roofs seemed to be continuous throughout the street. This cast an endless shadow on the district and made the muddy, crowded roads seem even more miserable but no less impressive.

Each of the houses were split into two. One family lived on the lower half, and another lived on the upper half. The upper half was the more desirable and expensive of the two, due to the sewer drains running along either side of the road the lower half of each house had a less pleasant smell throughout the year.

Apart from basic damages and decorations, each house seemed to be identical as you walked down the road. Some had pots of flowers outside the doors and some even had taken the time and care to paint the house in a different colour to the rest, however, due to the cost of this it was not a common sight.

Just as Jariko and the others were about to head through the next gate Jariko felt a hand on his shoulder. He turned around and saw a young man no older than he was in the same red tunic as the other guards, minus the armour and weapons.

"I understand you have information about the attack on Rybalin - Commander Claypius would like to speak to you urgently. If you would follow me please," the young guardsman said, waving his hand. He seemed too young and unsure of himself to be an experienced guard but Jariko still didn't want to offend him and with a slight nod agreed to follow him to see the commander.

"Jariko! Meet us at the George Inn tonight once you've settled your business. It's somewhere in the Market District," Mutana shouted as Jariko was quickly swept away by the young guard. Jariko paused and wanted to at least say goodbye to Kellarom and his brother, but the small group of mages seemed busy discussing the tournament, and most likely figuring out where they had to go. He would make a point of finding them later, so he pushed it out of his mind and headed off with the guard.

As he was quickly getting pulled through the magnificent city, Jariko found himself getting nervous and overwhelmed. He didn't know what he was going to say to Commander Claypius and as he rehearsed his story in his head, he couldn't help but be distracted as they passed through the second gate. The young guard quickly raised his right hand and placed a clenched fist onto his chest. This was their salute to one another to show respect to the higher-ranking guard, so Jariko copied as he passed the armoured man standing guard. He knew he looked silly, but he didn't care.

They entered the Market District, and all the buildings were the same as the housing district except every shop had a sign hanging above the door and market stands littered the road for as far as you could see, selling anything and everything they thought could get them a piece of gold. Jariko wanted to stop and wander around this district more, but he felt the young guard grab his arm and drag him onward.

"So, are you a guard?" Jariko asked knowing that he wasn't, but he felt he should make some conversation.

"No, I'm in my seventh year of training; it takes nine in total," the young guard replied sidestepping a group of kids that were playing in the road.

"How old are you?" Jariko asked.

"I'm seventeen. When I turn nineteen, I'll be knighted, for now I mainly do chores, clean armour and weapons and pass messages around the city."

This shocked Jariko. This boy was only a little older than he was and, in a few years, would be asked to die for his king and country.

"Am I allowed to ask your name?" Jariko asked, trying to figure out if he was annoying the young guard.

"Gregarous, but a kid like you can just call me Greg," Greg said turning back and giving Jariko a quick and subtle smile.

"Nice to meet you Greg, I'm Jariko."

"Pleasure," Greg replied as they approached the third gate into the Grand District, however, they didn't pass all the way through the gate, stopping halfway and going through a door built into the gate. A small corridor lay ahead dimly lit by torches. They were actually inside the wall.

Jariko never would have guessed the walls were hollow, but it makes sense and would be a lot easier to build.

"Are all the walls hollow?" Jariko asked.

"Only the second and third. Designed for ambushes and convenient use." This answer satisfied Jariko's curiosity and the two boys continued down the corridor, after a few minutes of walking they came to a door and Greg stopped, knocked on the door and before Jariko could thank him he jogged off.

"See you later Greg," Jariko yelled. Greg raised a hand but didn't turn or slow down. Jariko knocked on the door again and this time he heard a deep thunderous voice shout:

"Come in!"

Jariko composed himself and entered the room, standing over a table covered in papers, books and a small plate of food was a hulking man examining a map on Concorvia. When approaching him Jariko noticed crosses on different points of the map and one covering where Rybalin would be. The man looked up at Jariko and smiled.

"Ah you must be Jariko, come have a seat."

He walked around the table grabbing a small wooden chair and placing it in front of Jariko. At this point his nerves had got the better of him and he was lost in his own head and continued to stare at the Commander. He was a tall man towering over Jariko, with broad shoulders, huge arms and long blond hair done up in a bun on the top of his head, although a large scar covering the side of his head meant a large chunk of his hair was missing. He was wearing the same red tunic as the other guards but his chest plate was pleasantly decorated with engravings and patterns along the edges and a large lion's head in the centre which was the symbol of Concorvia and the Keepers.

“Come now, boy, I won't bite,” the Commander said letting out a joyful cackle. Jariko snapped himself out of his daze and took a seat. “I am Commander Claypius, but I suppose you already knew that.” Claypius said, cackling again and raising his hand to shake Jariko’s.

“M..my name is Jariko, sir,” Jariko said while shaking the Commander’s hand.

“Wow, strong handshake for a boy so young but please, no need for the sir nonsense, it's a pleasure to meet you Jariko. Now I understand you have information on the attack on Rybalin - my men have only just made it out there this morning so whatever information you have would be greatly appreciated.”

Jariko explained everything that had happened, trying not to show he was getting upset. He explained about the Roach-lins, the Ogres and the tunnels, as well as the queen that Blata had mentioned. His story seemed to disturb Claypius very deeply. The tunnels and the Ogres were likely the most worrying part and Claypius sat up and began to look over his map once again.

“And you say the tunnels led you all the way to the lake?” Claypius asked, pointing at the map.

“Yes si…Claypius.” Jariko replied. “I'm sorry, I can't be more useful.” Jariko added.

“No, no, this information will save lives Jariko, you have done very well. In fact I think the king himself should hear your story and thank you personally. None of my men have ever found these tunnels, let alone entered and exterminated the colony.”

This thought excited Jariko so much he jumped up in excitement to meet the king and then quickly realised where he was and composed himself, however, Claypius didn't seem to mind letting out another deep cackle.

“Give me a few days to report back to my superiors and I will see about your reward. Is there somewhere you are staying?” Claypius asked.

“Yes, the George Inn.”

“Ah, lovely place. Okay then, when I have more information, I'll send word to find you there.” Claypius leant forward to shake Jariko's hand again and Jariko shook it eagerly. Just as Jariko was about to leave Claypius spoke again.

"Oh, since you will be here for a few days, why don't you take these - I was planning on going myself but due to the attack, I'm far too busy."

He walked over to a small wooden box in the corner and pulled out a piece of paper and handed it to Jariko.

"A ticket to the tournament! Thank you so much," Jariko exclaimed, not believing his luck.

"Don't mention it, I shall see you in a few days. Goodbye Jariko," Claypius said smiling and waving, Jariko returned the wave and with a Cheshire grin he left the room with the ticket firmly in his hand.

Chapter Fifteen: The Tournament Begins

Jariko stepped through the door back out into the city and took a deep long breath of relief. He didn't know why he had worked himself up so much, but his anxiety had gotten the better of him, however, it was over now, and he had a ticket to the tournament. The thought of how he was going to watch the show had not occurred to him until this point, so it was a stroke of luck that Claypius had given him the ticket, nevertheless Jariko still had half the day left to explore the city and he wanted to make the most of it before finding the others at the inn later tonight. He decided to send word to old man Rolo as soon as possible so he headed to the Market District to find a messenger. After a little while of walking he saw a wooden sign that said *Sermos' Messenger Service*. Jariko entered the shop and saw a young man standing behind the counter.

"Welcome to Sermos' Messenger Service, the most trusted messenger service in all of Concorvia. We deliver as quick as a bird and safe as a lion - that's our motto. How can I help you." The boy spoke unnaturally quickly with a forced smile.

"I need to send a letter to a cabin north of Rybalin, here," Jariko said, pointing at a map roughly where his house should be.

"Not a problem, just write down your message and we will be on our way."

He handed Jariko a piece of paper and a pencil and Jariko wrote his letter. He purposely left out the danger and problems they had faced and just told Rolo he was safe and would be back home in a few weeks. He then handed to paper back to the young man.

"That will be two gold pieces please," the young man said. Jariko reached into his pocket but realised he only had silver pieces.

"I'm sorry but I don't have enough - but it's important, I need to make sure Rolo got home safe after the Rybalin attack!" Just as the young man was about to hand

Jariko's letter back to him, a man entered the room from a back door.

"Don't worry about the payment, I'm heading to Rybalin to send a message from the Commander, I don't mind taking a quick detour after that's done," the man said.

Jariko showed him on the map where his house was, and the man took his letter.

"Thank you so much!" Jariko exclaimed, but the man just smiled. He and Jariko left the shop together, but the man quickly started running to deliver the messages and was gone. Jariko couldn't believe his luck. He wandered back towards the Grand District gate not knowing what to do next.

He stood in between the Market District and the Grand District for a moment contemplating his choices, but found his eyes were becoming heavy. He took a swig of his medicine and stood there for a few minutes longer, torn on where he should start, until something in the corner of his eye caught his attention and he wandered into the Grand District.

In the distance of this open space within the city was a large spire towering over the walls and stabbing the heavens. Jariko recognised it immediately from the stories; it was the Cosilica. The physical representation of the unification of the Creators and mortals, it was the epicentre of worship and following of Primak and was now a symbol of hope and peace in all the land.

This cathedral outdated most of the city and even the palace had been built specifically to be near it. Some said it was the oldest building in Concorvia, however, the lack of aging or damage made it seem as if it was built only yesterday. The history and symbol of the city could only be outshone by the breath-taking design of the building itself, from the enormous stained-glass windows depicting the story of Primak, to the immense detail of every stone, brick, ledge and corner of the architecture, none of it could be described with words alone. The colossal wooden doors twenty feet tall were menacing as they swung slowly on their hinges to allow access to the sanctuary, however nothing compared to the two large, spiked towers on each corner at the front of the cathedral and largest tower rising from the centre, reaching all the way to the heavens.

Jariko followed the road with the tower growing larger and larger with every step. As he was walking, he took note of his surroundings. The Grand District was the largest district. Jariko could see small open fields, farms and houses on his left, mainly for the workers and suppliers to the palace and on his right, he could see the colosseum in the distance.

It was round and layered just like stacked cakes. As he got closer it grew in height dwarfing the building next to it. This was the main base and training grounds for Concorvia's armies. Jariko couldn't make out much of the details, but the roof was sloped as if it was an upside-down ship.

He decided to explore the barracks and colosseum later on and stayed true to his path to see the grand cathedral. Eventually he made it to the gate that was the entrance to the Harmony District and home to the

Cosilica. As he stepped through the gate he felt a chill run down his spine when he saw the endless sea of graves on his left, all different shapes, sizes and materials. Some had large statues of angels or animals while some had small buildings where a family could rest together in the afterlife, nevertheless these graves were a harsh reminder of death to Jariko and he didn't care for it, bringing memories of his mother to the front of his mind and harshly decreasing his jolly mood. He bowed his head and took a moment in her honour then proceeded to walk in the other direction to see the Cosilica and pretend like she was there with him, telling him one of his favourite stories or maybe one about the Cosilica itself.

Jariko's mother had always said that the Cosilica was built by one man, the first mage, Agorith. He supposedly built it all by himself and in less than an hour where Orkestra was originally located, when the old city was destroyed the Cosilica somehow disappeared and reappeared here, and this is why the new Orkestra was built in this location. Jariko didn't believe these stories when he was a child and even less now that he was here basking in its glory.

He approached the giant wooden doors and placed his hand on the oversized door handle and with a firm tug swung it open just enough for him to squeeze inside then closed the door behind him. He took a few steps in silence, and proceeded to view the interior, awestruck, and lost for words.

The first thing that caught his eye was an orb floating high in the ceiling shining a pale light onto every surface in the room. The orb was large in size and emitting a crisp white light, but when looking straight at it, it didn't seem to hurt or blind you, almost as if it dimmed itself for the beholder. It was covered in strange markings that hypnotically twirled as the orb rotated slowly in mid-air. Jariko's gaze slowly drifted downwards, and he found himself looking at a large statue of a man with both arms stretched out in front of him. From where he was standing it almost looked like the statue was casting a spell that suspended the orb in the air. The statue was surrounded by dozens of candles and flowers - tributes to the gods or prayers to be heard. As Jariko approached the statue, he momentarily lingered, trying to decide if he should light a candle and pray for his mother, his good health or something else, But he found himself struggling to do so; his faith in the Creators and their divine plans had waned since his mother's death. He felt that the part of him that optimistically and ignorantly trusted the Creators was buried with his mother. He found that he could only trust himself, his friends, and the choices that they made, unaffected by a Creator's will. Jariko felt rage build up inside himself and just as he started to feel overwhelmed, he heard a deep and cracking voice that scattered his thoughts with surprise.

"It's hard to face him with a heavy heart," said the old voice. Jariko wiped a tear from his face with his hand before turning round.

"I'm sorry?" He asked, confused.

"The statue is of Agorith, the first Grandmaster and founder of our order," the man said stepping out from a dim doorway and into the light. He was an old man with combed back white hair and a beard that dangled down to his chest. He was wearing robes similar to Irabella and Mutana however he wore a large poncho much like Jariko's. It was in much better condition and a deep red colour decorated with beautiful patterns that flowed down from the hood and covered the entire poncho. He continued to talk as he walked over to Jariko.

"No one knows why but any who stand in the presence of this statue have to face their deepest struggles and darkest shames," the old man stopped once he was standing right next to Jariko no less than arm's length away. He turned and smiled with a soft and kind face even though time had not been kind to him. "It is hard to face the things we bury deep inside ourselves, but once we overcome them we are reborn with new purpose, and once a person has the strength to stand here and not be crippled by their demons they leave a candle or flower to give thanks. The candles will never go out and the flowers will never wilt, and the person will never be the same again."

Jariko was curious and more than a little confused but before he could respond the man turned around and walked away still smiling.

He thought about what the old man had said and tried to make sense of it, but once again he found images of his mother were flooding his mind. After a few moments he composed himself and tore himself away from the statue. He walked straight to the door refusing to look back and tried to clear his mind. He pushed the door open with a shove and slammed it shut behind him.

Once outside he composed himself and leant up against the wall of the Cosilica.

What demons do I hold onto, why am I filled with such guilt and shame? Jariko thought. Frustrated, he forced himself to think of other things and walked at a rapid pace away from the cathedral.

Jariko found himself back in the Grand District. Still disturbed by his encounter he tried desperately to think of anything else, when suddenly, the ground shook with a mighty rumble and a deafening bang making him stagger as he walked. He looked over in the direction of the colosseum and saw a plume of smoke climbing into the sky. Jariko broke out into a run to see what the noise was. There were a few people walking the same road he was on, however the explosion merely caught their attention and nothing more. No one seemed to share his panic and he almost felt silly running. His run slowed to a jog and then to a brisk walk when he noticed a small crowd of people around the epicentre of the blast.

Jariko realised what and where he was: this was the training camp and most likely where all the traveling mages were getting ready for the tournament tomorrow. He joined the crowd but couldn't see anything due to his below average height. He began pushing and slipping in between all the people and slowly made his way to the front and found himself pinned to a metal railing separating the people from the mages.

It was Kellarom training with his brother. The two were fiercely battling, landing hits one after the other. Kellarom was wielding the staff he had worn on his back, but his brother had no weapons, only a brutish golem made of sand and stones standing next to him.

Wow, Jariko thought. He had never seen a real golem before. Creation magic was a rarer form in this part of the country, so it was a privilege to witness.

The fight continued for a while, Kellarom slowing down as it did until his legs began to shake and his strength waned. In a last-ditch effort, Kellarom stopped, composed himself and waved his hand over his staff. As he did, a dull blue light formed around the staff and took the shape of a blade; this would be his final attack. He pulled the weapon back and in one mighty motion he swung the blade of pure energy but he didn't move, instead a crystal coloured shock wave hurtled towards his brother. Then, as it hit him, a large cloud of dust enveloped the arena and some of the people watching. The arena fell silent. The dust started to settle and Jariko could see Kellarom on one knee. He had a smile on his face waiting to see if his final attack had worked. The smile quickly disappeared when a large shadow became visible in the sand cloud. Everyone could see it: a twenty-foot-tall humanoid monster made of stone. It was no more than a torso, with no legs or limbs, like a giant Golem in half. Standing inside was Moritus smirking without a scratch. This giant half Golem had protected him from the blast.

Amazing! To think he could make something that big, Jariko thought. He looked back over to Kellarom who was chuckling to himself before falling on his back still laughing.

"Well done brother, but I thought you would at least keep the spells simple for me," he shouted.

"Says the guy who used an energy blade attack - you could have killed me!" Moritus replied climbing out of the giant torso before it began to crumble and fall apart. He walked over to his brother and held out his hand. Kellarom grabbed it and stood up as the crowd exploded with applause. The two brothers bowed before walking over to some rocks where they left their bags. The crowd began to disperse and Jariko made his way over to see them.

"That was amazing!" Jariko exclaimed as he approached them.
"Oh, hey Jariko, I didn't realise you were here. So, what do you think? We're pretty good, right?" Kellarom said, winking.

"Moritus was! He wiped the floor with you," Jariko said and Moritus laughed. Kellarom didn't seem as amused.

"I could take you on any day of the week!" Kellarom said standing to look at Jariko in the eye. Jariko smirked.

"Bring it," he replied. Then the two started laughing.

"On second thought, let's do it tomorrow," Kellarom said, grabbing his side and sitting back down.

"Where are the other two?" Moritus asked.

"I'm not sure, I haven't seen them since I left you guys at the main gate."

“Well, wish Mutana good luck from me, I hope we don't have to fight tomorrow,” Moritus said joining his brother.

“I would hate to embarrass her,” Moritus said this with a cheeky smile and Jariko knew he meant nothing by it.

“Are you ready?” Jariko asked.

“As ready as I'll ever be, but this tournament is never simple.”

“How come?”

“The last time they held it there were three rounds, but each round was completely different. They aren't looking for just the strongest but the smartest and wisest, so they make strange tests to assess different parts of us to see who's best for the position of Grandmaster, as well as the exam we have to take at the beginning,” Moritus explained.

“So, you have no idea what you have to do tomorrow?”

“Correct.”

This made the tournament that much more exciting for Jariko.

“Well, after a warmup like that I could do with a bath, then a good night's sleep,” Moritus said standing back up. “Come on, Kellarom.”

“It's not even dark yet!?” Kellarom stated. This was true; there was still at least another few hours of daylight left.

“If I have to sleep, I can't be worrying about what you're doing, so come on. We’ll see you tomorrow Jariko,"

Moritus said smiling as he picked his bag up from the ground and brushed the dust off of it.

"See you later Jariko," Kellarom said like a child stropping.

"See you guys later, good luck for tomorrow," Jariko waved them goodbye, but he had no plans to go to sleep yet.

He headed back to the Market District, thinking about the battle he just watched and getting more and more excited about how much more he was going to see tomorrow. Jariko spent a few hours in the Market District, wandering around every shop he could find. He had no money, but he liked to see what was for sale. He did this until his legs started to ache and his eyes became heavy, and he decided to head to the George Inn to meet Irabella and Mutana.

He found the two of them having some food outside the inn and he joined them. After eating and catching up on the day's events, the three of them headed to bed. Just like the night before, Mutana insisted she paid for Jariko, and she rented two rooms. The three of them said good night and retired to bed. The tournament was imminent and within minutes of parting all three were sound asleep.

Morning broke and rays of light peeped through the curtains of Jarikos' room and woke him up. He made his way down the stairs and out the front door. The morning air was crisp and refreshing as he took a deep breath. After having some breakfast, he saw Irabella walk down the stairs.

"Where's Mutana?" Jariko asked looking around the room in case he hadn't noticed her sitting there.

"She's already gone. She left just before sunrise and said to meet her at the colosseum," Irabella replied.

"Oh, okay. Wanna have some breakfast then head out?" Jariko said, pushing a plate of sausages and eggs towards her that he had already ordered.

"No, I'm fine, thank you. I'm too nervous to eat - can we just head out?" Irabella asked, seemingly feeling bad that Jariko had gone through the effort of getting her breakfast. However, Jariko didn't mind and with a smile nodded. He grabbed the sausages and began eating one as he picked up his bag and the two left for the colosseum. The sun had almost reached its peak in the sky by the time they reached the starting ceremony. The crowd was enormous and took up most of the area surrounding the colosseum. Irabella found an opening of the crowd with two guards at the entrance. They both showed their tickets and made their way into the colosseum. They decided to sit at the top to get the best view of the first event, however, they quickly regretted this decision as the stairs seemed endless. Eventually, they reached the summit.

They stood at the top of the stairs and then heard: "Jariko! Irabella!" It was Kellarom, he was waving them over to his table where he had saved them two seats.

"Thank you," Irabella said softly.

"Don't mention it. Its just lucky you guys had the same idea to come to the top," Kellarom chuckled, but before

Jariko could say anything in reply they heard a thunderous voice call for silence. They looked down and saw an old man standing in the centre of the colosseum.

"That's the Grandmaster!" Irabella shouted in excitement as the colosseum erupted in applause. Jariko was stunned when he realised it was the same old man from the Cosilica.

"Quiet please, quiet down." The colosseum died down to a light clap and then to silence.

"Welcome one and all to our magnificent city. I am the Grandmaster of the Church of Primak and head of the magic council that protects this city and our grand country. It has been my privilege and pleasure to serve all of you, however, this job has taken a toll on me and now I am getting to an age where I am no longer able to lead how you deserve. For this reason I have chosen to host this tournament and as our tradition states this will be where I shall find my replacement." The crowd erupted once again and he paused for a moment before continuing.

"However, this tournament is not for the faint-hearted. It will push our contenders to their limits and beyond." As he said this the mages participating entered the arena and once again the crowd erupted into applause, Jariko could see Mutana in the line and Moritus next to her standing proud and dignified.

"Take a good look, for one of these fine men or women will be chosen to be my successor. I wish you nothing, but luck and I hope that every single one of you will show us your best. I look forward to seeing what you are all made of. Stay safe and enjoy!" The Grandmaster gave a wave and left the arena while an Elf took his place. He was a much younger, well-dressed mage and had the yellow skin of a Forgotten Elf, as well as the pointed ears.

"My name is Sheladon and I shall be the assessor of the tournament. If the participants will please follow me into the examination room for the written exam, unfortunately we cannot have spectators for this round, but we look forward to seeing you all for the first round later today." The crowd seemed disappointed but knew this was the first step of the tournament. A large portion of the crowd began to leave not wanting to wait, but the remaining spectators including Jariko, Irabella and Kellarom stayed not wanting to lose their seats. Jariko didn't mind the wait. The excitement was almost too much for him and he could barely contain it. The tournament had finally begun, history was about to be made and he was about to watch it unfold.

Chapter Sixteen: Unexpected Turn

Jariko and Kellarom spent the next few hours telling bad jokes, stories, and showing off weird tricks that Kellarom had learnt, including the strange talent of sticking a long nail up his nose. It was extraordinary to watch and strangely hypnotic for Jariko, Irabella, however, was not impressed, burying her nose deeper and deeper into the book she had brought and snidely tutting at the two boys in disgust. This didn't bother the two of them who were quickly becoming close friends and seemed to have a lot in common. They sat chatting and joking with each other but after a while they became hungry and Kellarom stood up.

“I'll be right back,” he exclaimed, still laughing at a joke Jariko had just told him. When he returned, he was carrying a pile of food he had ordered using most of the gold Moritus had given him. It was a collection of bread, cheese, meat and sweets that he found in the small market that had been built outside the main entrance.

“You really didn't have to do that!” Irabella said putting her book down.

“Don’t worry about it,” he leaned in to whisper. “It’s my brother's money.” He pulled back and winked at Irabella. Jariko pretended not to notice but he had a sickening feeling of jealousy in his stomach. He could never be that cool or confident around Irabella. Not wanting to be shown up, Jariko looked at Kellarom.

“I bet I can eat more than you,” Jariko stated proudly. Kellarom paused before a large grin enveloped his face.

“You’re on,” he replied before grabbing a handful of bread and slamming it into his mouth. Rolling her eyes, Irabella took a plate and grabbed as much food as she would need before leaning back with the book suspended in the air with magic in front of her face while she ate. This would have impressed Jariko, if he had noticed. After only minutes, all the bread, meats and cheeses were gone and all that was left were the sweets: golden brown sweet rolls and little cakes. Jariko began devouring whatever he could reach. His inhuman appetite was unheard of but Kellarom was slowing down. All the bread and cheese had taken its toll on him and after a few minutes he conceded.

"What even are you?!" Kellarom struggled to say with his mouth full before slumping his head back to rest. Jariko jumped up with his mouth still full, cheering and celebrating. His victory was short lived however for a few moments later the doors to the examination room swung open and Jariko paused to see who would emerge.

Sheladon was first to appear and following him were the mages, although the group had significantly decreased to only eight of the twenty that had entered. Irabella cheered as she saw Mutana step out into the sunlight Jariko joined her and so did Kellarom when he saw Moritus step out. The eight remaining contestants stood in the centre of the arena before Sheladon spoke.

"The first stage of the tournament is complete!" He exclaimed triumphantly. "These are the remaining contestants who successfully scored over the ninety percent pass mark," he said, waving his hands towards the contestants.

"They achieved the ninety percent mark needed to proceed onto the next event. However, this is only the beginning. From here, these powerful mages will face three more of the toughest challenges that we can only pray they are ready for."

As he was saying this, a young man ran up to Sheladon with a small bucket and handed it to him before running back. Sheladon walked over to the mages, and they all stuck their hand into the bucket and pulled out what looked like crumpled bits of paper. Then, Sheladon addressed the crowd one more time.

"The previous challenge pushed the mages to show the limits of their minds. This challenge will push the limits of their body. A one-on-one fight between mages. We have an even number, so at the end of this challenge only four will remain. To make this fair for everyone the mages have just pulled a random piece of paper with a number on it." The crowd seemed confused.

"We will work our way through the battles determined by these numbers. Number one and number two, will you please stay in the arena and can the other mages please go and wait inside for your number to be called." The mages who were not battling began to make their way back to the door they had entered from. Mutana and Moritus were both walking back so they were not fighting this round.

"I wonder if they will be fighting each other?" Irabella said, worried.

"You're just worried 'cause you know my brother's magic is effective against Mutana's and she won't be able to beat him," Kellarom exclaimed proudly.

"It's not just that. I was hoping they both would make it further into the competition."

“I agree,” Jariko said, “It would suck if either of them got kicked out this early,” Jariko looked at Irabella for approval, but she was distracted by the two mages still in the arena.

“Yeah, whatever, my brother is gonna win anyway so there's no need to worry about him.”

Just before Jariko had a chance to reply with what would most likely be an insult, a thunderous voice shouted: “Begin!” and the two mages flew into a rage. Jariko had never seen people fight with such ferocity.

“They’re gonna kill each other if they aren't careful,” Jariko exclaimed. He was mesmerised by the flashing lights and small explosions caused by various fireballs and lightning strikes.

“That's all part of the risk Jariko, this is a deadly competition to find the strongest mage. People can die and have died. It's the risk you have to take to become Grandmaster,” Irabella explained.

This shocked Jariko - the thought of that sweet old man having to go through this and even killing someone just didn't seem right, however, the things he had witnessed mages doing over the last few days, it was no surprise they needed to make it such a challenge to find the best among all these gifted people.

Everyone in the crowd was mesmerised by the fight happening in front of them. It was rare to see two mages fight at this level. No one could stop watching until the fight was over and one mage stood victorious over the other. He wasn't dead but badly injured and exhausted. The winner stuck both his hands into the air in triumph.

"Toral wins!" Sheladon exclaimed and the crowd exploded into applause.

"He's from Orkestra, trained right here under the Grandmaster himself. It's no wonder he won," Kellarom explained, but Jariko and Irabella didn't hear him because they were watching as the next two mages stepped out into the arena. It was Mutana and another mage they didn't know.

"That's lucky for Mutana," Kellarom said in a cocky way, annoyed that they ignored him. They still weren't paying attention and began to cheer for Mutana.

"Did you say something?" Jariko said smirking as he sat back down. Kellarom punched him in the arm and they laughed.

"SHHH!" Irabella said in frustration. "It's starting."

All three of them leant forward in anticipation.

"Begin!"

Before anyone could react, Mutana let out a large spray of flames from her mouth. The other mage began running in circles around Mutana but she and the flames followed him. The flames were biting at his heels before he raised his hand and all the large stones in the arena began to rise up from the floor. Mutana saw what was coming and leaped into a roll out of the way before all the stones shot down at high speeds from all directions, directly where she was standing. This caused a large plume of dust to fill the arena. It was still for a moment before a blazing light flew into the sky then slowed down and then began plummeting back down. Six more fireballs were shot into the sky before Jariko lost count.

“That's Mutana’s hell storm!” Irabella shouted.

They all watched as the mage threw large boulders at the fire in an attempt to blow them up before they hit the ground, however, this was futile as the first fire ball hit the ground in a magnificent explosion dispersing some of the dust and revealing the other mage as he was thrown back from the shock wave. Mutana leaped out and began to fight the mage in hand-to-hand combat while effortlessly dodging the raining fire above her.

Just as the last fireball was about to hit the ground, Mutana struck the mage and he flinched. This gave her the opportunity to grab and throw the poor mage directly into the line of the fireball, exploding on contact and winning the match. The same doctors from before came rushing out expecting the worst but were pleasantly surprised to see that he was still alive.

“Mutana’s hell storm isn't actually dangerous. To make them last so long in the air and fall back down she has to significantly decrease the heat to make sure they don't burn out too soon,” Irabella explained. “The explosion probably still hurt but he won’t have any major burns.”

“She's amazing!” Jariko shouted, getting excited.

“She’s gonna need more than party tricks like that to stop my brother,” Kellarom said.

"Well, let's see if he even makes it any further, shall we?" Irabella said, pointing down to the arena. Kellarom looked and saw Moritus entering.

"Go Moritus!" He shouted, jumping out of his seat. Moritus looked up at Kellarom and instead of his normal smile the three of them only saw fear in Moritus before he looked back down at his opponent. The three of them looked at each other with worried looks.

"He's just nervous," Kellarom said, but even he did not seem convinced by that sentiment.

After a few moments Kellarom looked at Jariko. "Something's wrong, we have to stop this fight."

Jariko and Irabella looked at each other before nodding. They all had a strange feeling but before they could all stand up, Sheladon had shouted "Begin!"

The fight began, but this didn't stop Kellarom. He jumped out of his seat and started making his way to the stairs. Jariko and Irabella followed. The colosseum was filled with people so they struggled to make their way through. Eventually they got to the stairs. They could hear the loud crashes and they could feel the ground shake every few seconds. Most likely from one of Moritus' golems. Just as they made it to the next floor they could hear cheering and Jariko saw a small gap in the crowd. The other mage was using swords made of magic just like Kellarom did with his staff.

Why would Moritus be so nervous if he knew his opponent's magic wouldn't be effective against him? Jariko thought to himself as they carried on down the stairs. The tremors in the ground and the roar of the crowd grew louder and louder before they finally made it to the ground floor and started making their way over to where Sheladon, the Grandmaster and a few other high ranking mages were sitting watching the battle.

The crowd was getting harder and harder to move through and the three of them found themselves getting split up. Jariko had no idea where the others had gone and he wasn't tall enough to see over people's heads. He just kept pushing in the same direction and getting more and more angry looks as he did so. Suddenly the crowd roared again, so loud it stunned Jariko for a moment. Then he heard shouting from the arena. He pushed forward until he was in the front row of the crowd and saw Moritus with a single golem and the other mage with his magic sword.

The mage began to focus on his sword and he was shouting almost as if it was hurting him, then the sword began to grow in size and glowed brighter than before. Jariko knew what was coming, it was the same move Kellarom used when he launched the magic at Moritus when they were sparring. The mage let out an almighty scream and threw his glowing blade at Moritus, and as he did, it turned into a shockwave of power. He raised his hand and, just like before, the explosion caused a large dust cloud that filled the arena. No one could see and the colosseum was silent. Jariko waited to see the shadow of his giant golem torso to appear in the dust, but it never came. The dust began to settle and then people began to understand when the same doctors from the previous fights charged into the arena.

That means the fight's over but who won? Jariko thought. He heard Kellarom scream from a few metres away from him, so loud it echoed around the colosseum and the crowd watched in horror as they saw Kellarom jump down into the arena to his brother's lifeless body. The energy blast had made direct contact and killed him instantly. Kellarom pushed the doctors away from Moritus' body and fell to his knees pulling his brother up onto his lap. The whole crowd was silent as they watched Kellarom cry for his lost brother. The victorious mage Paralom walked over to Kellarom and placed a hand on his shoulder. Kellarom stuck his hand out towards him while a blue magic blade materialised in Kellarom's hand. Paralom raised his hands in the air in peace.

"I'm sorry, but he knew the risks," Paralom said, before leaving the arena. Jariko jumped into the arena to get Kellarom, but he wouldn't let go of his brother's body.

"Come on, Kell," Jariko said, wrapping his arm around him. "Let's do this inside."

Kellarom nodded and the doctors carried the body away. Something still didn't feel right to Jariko, but he pushed the thoughts away and focused on helping his friend, he and Kellarom followed the doctor's inside to mourn their loss.

Chapter Seventeen: Questions

Jariko and Kellarom sat silently in the waiting room with Mutana and were soon joined by Irabella. The only noise was from Kellarom, still crying, clutching a necklace he had around his neck. None of the group knew what to say. They just sat there in silence while the final battle continued on. Jariko knew exactly what Kellarom was going through; he had not lost a brother, but he was with his mother when she died. He knew how much it hurts. Even so, he couldn't find the right words to say - he knew words wouldn't really help. After a few minutes the crowd's applause filled the room; the first round was complete. The sound angered Kellarom. He flew into a rage, grabbed an empty chair next to him and throwing it into the wall.

"They don't even care!" He screamed, falling to his knees and beginning to cry again.

Jariko stood up and walked to Kellarom placing a hand on his shoulder.

"They didn't know him - to them this is just entertainment," Mutana said. "These are the risks we take when we sign up. Moritus knew that."

"Moritus was the strongest mage here, he shouldn't have died like that," Kellarom replied, anger filling his voice.

"It's true," Jariko said. "We all saw his face before the match started, something was wrong, plus Kellarom did the same move to him when they sparred, and he blocked it without breaking a sweat. It doesn't make sense."

Before Mutana could respond, the door opened, and the Grandmaster stepped into the room. He paused for a moment. He didn't say a word, but his face said it all. It was one of sadness and exhaustion. Jariko could tell he had to do this one too many times. How can you empathise with someone when their loved ones die for a silly tradition? The pain on his face was as if he lost his own brother. He walked up to Kellarom, knelt down and looked him in the eyes.

"Come with me," he said in his deep but welcoming voice. "You too, Jariko," he added. Jariko was surprised but started walking without hesitation. He led them out of the room and down several long corridors before getting to a strange trap door at the bottom of a dead end.

"Be a good lad Jariko and open the hatch," the Grandmaster said. Confused, Jariko followed his instructions and opened the hatch. It revealed a ladder leading down into a dark tunnel and the Grandmaster began to make his way down. Jariko was getting flashbacks to the Roach-lins tunnels as he made the climb down the ladder. Once all three were in the tunnel the Grandmaster clicked his fingers and a small flame lit up on his finger. He pulled a torch from the wall and lit it. The light showed the darkness for what it was: a dirt tunnel with large concrete slabs on the floor creating a path.

They followed silently as the three of them walked this dark and wet path. Jariko looked over to Kellarom - his head was looking down at the ground with dried tears staining his face. He wanted to ask where they were going but restrained himself. The silence seemed intentional. After a while of walking, they got to another ladder. Jariko climbed up and opened the hatch at the top. Once he escaped the tunnel he realised where they were, he was back in the Cosilica. He recognised the walls and the smell of the building; however, he didn't know where in the Cosilica they were. The Grandmaster was next to emerge followed by Kellarom.

Still confused, Jariko asked, "Why are we here? And why is there a tunnel here?"

"All in good time," the Grandmaster responded before walking up a spiralling staircase. Jariko was beginning to get tired. The food he had eaten earlier that day wasn't enough. He quickly took a drink of his medicine while climbing the stairs and just as he returned it to his bag he found himself standing outside a great wooden door.

"This is a secret entrance to my library. Only the greatest mages I deem worthy may enter my private library, or even know of its existence, although they usually use the main door."

As he said this he pushed the great wooden doors and they squealed open revealing a large hall filled from top to bottom with books, scrolls and tapestries. As distraught as he was even Kellarom couldn't help but be amazed by the wealth of knowledge here. The Grandmaster finally sat down at a large table in the centre of the circular room, with the two boys sat opposite him. Kellarom seemed a little more aware of the strange situation and was curious about what was happening.

"I'm sorry, Kellarom. I can't imagine what that was like for you. I can only hope you will forgive me for hosting this harsh tournament."

"I don't blame you, Grandmaster," Kellarom replied, holding back more tears.

"Please call me Merlon."

"Um, Mr. Merlon. Why did you bring us here?" Jariko asked.

"If Kellarom tried to leave through one of the main entrances he would have been bombarded with questions and most likely some unsavoury comments. The least I could do was spare him that. As far as you're concerned, it seemed like Kellarom would need a friend." Merlon stood up as he continued talking. "This tournament has been held many times over the years, trying to find a worthy successor for myself. However, accidents like this do happen and it breaks my heart to know it is my fault."

Kellarom jumped out of his seat and slammed his fist on the table.

"This was no accident!" He shouted, startling Merlon. "Something was off about that match. My brother should not have died so easily!" Kellarom broke down into tears once more and sat back down.

"Kell's right - I know Moritus was a better mage than that," Jariko added. Merlon seemed to consider this for a moment before speaking.

"He did score the best in the exam out of all the other mages, almost beating my perfect record. It does seem strange that he couldn't counter a simple attack," Merlon stroked his beard as he contemplated this thought more. "So, what do you suggest happened?" He added.

Jariko and Kellarom looked at each other. Neither had any idea what was wrong with him during the match.

"What if your brother intended to lose the match?" Merlon asked, but this didn't sit well with Kellarom.

"My brother wouldn't kill himself!" Kellarom shouted back. "He had a girl waiting for him at home. He wanted to spend his life with her. He told me that himself. There's no way he would do that to me either, plus he always dreamed of being Grandmaster."

The room fell silent; no one wanted to speak after hearing that. It was almost as if the realisation of Moritus having a life and dreams made his death that much harder to accept. They sat at the table for a few minutes, then Merlon spoke.

"We have been searching for a specific criminal that might have been able to force Moritus' hand," Merlon said in deep thought.

"Sireana!" Jariko shouted. Kellarom looked at him confused. "On her wanted poster it said she had the ability to make men do whatever she wanted. What if she's here in the city and forced Moritus to kill himself?" Jariko explained.

"Why would she do something like that?" Kellarom said.

"Who knows? But if she is here we might have a chance to find her!"

Kellarom's rage was growing. His fists began to clench tighter as the urge for vengeance grew. Merlon, however, hadn't said anything and still seemed to be contemplating the idea.

"How could she control him? Perception magic isn't that powerful," Kellarom asked.

"No, but an artifact would be," Merlon added, joining the conversation. The two young boys seemed confused.

"Artifact?" Jariko asked.

"Many years ago, back when magic was first discovered by Agorith, he also discovered a way to enchant objects, by harnessing Pure magic he could fuse a large amount of magic to an object, unlocking its full potential on our plane of existence. In other words, it could bend reality in strange ways."

Merlon stood up from his chair and walked over to a dust covered bookshelf. He looked over the spines of the books for a moment before pulling out a large book. He walked back over to the table and put the large book down with a loud thud. After flicking through the book for a few minutes he found the page he was looking for and spun the book around to show Jariko and Kellarom. Jariko's eyes darted to the detailed picture of a sword, encrusted with jewels and strange runes running down the blade. It was a strange sword to say the least.

"This is the sword of the Cosilica, forged for a king in the ancient times. It was enchanted by Agorith for the king. Once enchanted this sword could cut through anyone in one swing. You see, a sword is made to cut through creatures or armour, and where a normal sword is limited by its material or sharpness, a sword fused with Pure magic does not obey our world's logic and so becomes able to cut through anything as if it were butter. Pure magic is what the Creators used to create everything, so an object infused with their power does not conform to the laws of our reality and because of this it becomes the greatest version of itself." Merlon stopped to judge how much the two boys were taking in; they seemed confused.

"I can see you still don't get it so think of it like this: everything is made with a purpose and naturally, is limited by the laws of reality and common sense, but if you imbue it with Pure magic, the same magic that Creators themselves use, then it doesn't have to conform to this world's laws of logic, just like the Creators who come from a completely different reality. You harness a small amount of the power of the Gods when wielding an enchanted Artifact. Therefore, for the short time enchanting was legal, countless artifacts were made. All of the most powerful people known in history wielded some kind of enchantment, that's why we try to record every enchanted item we are aware of."

The thought of such items being around the world struck Jariko; all he wanted to do was learn more.

"Sir, you said it's not legal to enchant these things anymore, why is that?"

"Good question, Jariko. You see, the rise of these artifacts caused a large shift in power for the countries and even the cities within them. Every power in the world was searching for them or creating their own and many wars and civil wars broke out. So, because of this, the council of Titans, which is made up of the five most powerful people in all the lands, was created. They declared that enchanting would become illegal. However, this decision itself caused a war - the battles to collect the artifacts were long and gruesome and they stretched for many years. Eventually the art of enchanting was locked away deep in this very building, to be guarded by the most powerful mage of the most powerful land. That is one of my main jobs here," Merlon said.

"How does this have anything to do with Sireana and my brother?" Kellarom shouted out of frustration. Merlon nodded and began flicking through his large book once again before stopping. It was a long list with many rows of items and numbers.

"This is the list of every artifact that the church has discovered or learned about, even artifacts in stories and songs. Each artifact is organised by a Category system.

Category one being an item that affects itself and its condition in minor ways, Category two items affect themselves and other objects in minor ways, Category three items affect people's minds in major ways,

Category four items affect the physical structure of an object or a person and force drastic changes and Category five are items that change reality for people and objects in major ways. As far as we're aware, Category Five items don't have a limit to their capabilities. Every category is powerful in its own way, and each were misused causing the art of enchanting to be forbidden and lost throughout the world."

Jariko was confused by all this new information but began to understand as Merlon gave him examples of each category. He couldn't help but become entranced in this topic as he made his way down the list.

"Torch-never goes out- category one

chain-never breaks-category one

Key-opens any door-category two

Paint brush-creates greatest art-category two

Cloak-wearer becomes invisible-category three

Mask-causes extreme fear-category three

Medicine-heals any wound-category four

Sword-can cut through anything living-category four

Bow-never misses-category five

Shield-withstand any attack-category five"

The list went on and on. Merlon pointed to a specific entry in the list.

"Jewelled necklace-wearer becomes most beautiful-category three"

Kellarom was confused.

"I still don't understand."

"The Jewels of beauty were lost many years ago, but this Artifact was particularly dangerous. The wearer somehow gains control of any person who is even slightly attracted to them through a forced love obsession. They see the wearer as a goddess, the victim of the wielder has no choice but to do what their love tells them to do."

"Just like the wanted posters say about Sireana Silvertongue - she must have this Artifact?!" Kellarom shouted, finally understanding.

"So, that means she must have been at the arena today and told Moritus to lose the match." Jariko was sickened by this realisation. The thought of Moritus being aware he was going to die while fighting broke Jariko's heart.

"We need to find her!" Kellarom shouted, "I'm gonna kill her!" His blood was boiling and it was directed at Sireana.

"Calm down now, Kellarom," Merlon preached.

"How do you suppose we find her? No one knows what she looks like and even the guards haven't been able to find a single clue to lead them to her. It's too dangerous for two young boys to go snooping around after a dangerous criminal. I won't allow it."

The room fell silent. Merlon's tone scared Kellarom into calming down and Jariko was still quietly thinking.

"What if we just figured out who she was, then the Commander and his guards could go and get her. Maybe she won't be so cautious around two boys and maybe she will make a mistake," Jariko suggested.

"And how do you suppose you can help find her?" Merlon asked, curious at Jariko's confidence. Jariko pondered this question for a moment before answering.

"Well, she must be here for a reason, right? If we could figure out what she's here for, maybe we can figure out what she's doing next, then beat her to it."

Merlon pondered this for a moment.

"And what do you think she's here for?" Merlon asked.

"No one could possibly know… but even if she is here for a greater purpose, what if she still acts like a common criminal?" Kellarom added.

"I don't follow," Merlon said, stroking his beard once again.

"If she's trying to control the outcome of the tournament for whatever reason, what criminal could resist betting on that person? They could double their money."

Jariko became excited.

"So, all we have to do is go down to the betting man and see who placed the largest bet and that's our suspect!" Jariko added and Kellarom grabbed Jariko's shoulder.

"Exactly!"

"Calm down you two, I can't allow you to go running after a dangerous criminal, especially you Kellarom. Whatever you're planning on doing is not going to work and she will kill you," Merlon said while standing up, his tone was serious and little frightening for the two boys.

"I refuse to sit around and let her kill anyone else! I'm going!" Kellarom shouted, exploding from his chair and running to the main door. Merlon shook his head in disappointment.

"Go with him Jariko, I feel if anyone can keep him safe right now it's you."

Jariko nodded before running after Kellarom.

Chapter Eighteen: The Stranger

It had been almost an hour since Jariko and Kellarom went with the Grandmaster, Irabella and Mutanna still sat waiting for any news or for the boys to return. Irabella's curiosity was too much, and she decided to try and find them.

"Where are you going?" Mutana asked.

"I wanna see where they went - they couldn't have left the Colosseum," Irabella replied, picking up her bag from the ground.

"I'll come with you - don't want you walking around on your own if what Jariko said was true."

"I believe him. Something was wrong with Moritus, I could see it in his eyes," Irabella responded wiping a tear that was running down her cheek.

"We can't just start saying that he was murdered without any evidence or facts. Once the tournament ends we will have a better chance of finding something out."

Irabella shook her head.

"But it will be too late by then - what if someone else gets killed? That death would be on our hands," Irabella preached, trying not to get emotional.

"Let's just worry about Kellarom for now. He just watched his brother die and nothing can change that. I can't imagine what he's going through. Let's just try and find them."

This made sense to Irabella; she didn't want to admit it to Mutana, but she knew that she was right. Kellarom was her friend and she needed to make sure he was okay first. Besides, she knew that she would need Jariko's help. She had started to get used to relying on him and she enjoyed his company. Irabella didn't really like people this much, so this was a nice change.

After twenty minutes of aimlessly walking, they found an empty corridor that didn't seem to go anywhere. They could see the end and there was no door or other corridor, it just ended. They decided to investigate it anyway and they walked to the end. Once they were there, they could see a strange hatch in the floor. It was completely hidden unless you walked up to it and this piqued their curiosity.

"Do you think they went down there?" Irabella asked, lifting the hatch.

Mutana climbed down and saw the dirt tunnel that the Grandmaster had led Jariko and Kellarom down.

"Why would the Colosseum have a secret tunnel?" Irabella asked.

"Many years ago, there was a war with the Shatorems of the east. Evil pirates that were upset by the sea taxes the king at the time had put on them demanded that they shouldn't have to pay and began smuggling things into the country. Once the king found out he was very angry and had his fleet sink any Shatorem ship that sailed on the west coast. In fear of the pirates breaking into the city the king had dozens of escape routes dug all around the city. I'm betting this is one of them. It probably leads to the palace or maybe the Cosilica, who knows, but these tunnels are forbidden so if they did go down here, we can’t follow them. But it's good that we found one though." Mutana climbed out of the tunnel and brushed herself off not wanting her white robes to be dirty and they left. Irabella was beginning to feel anxious; she had no idea where Jariko and Kellarom were. Mutana could see the worry on her face and put her arm around her.

"Don't worry Bella. They are with the Grandmaster; nothing is going to happen to them. We can meet up with them tonight at the inn," Mutanna said smiling. Irabella smiled back and they headed to the exit of the colosseum.

They left with the swarm of other spectators leaving the colosseum. Irabella still wasn't feeling right and the large crowd wasn't helping.

"So, what do you need to prepare for tomorrow?" She asked Mutana, trying to distract herself.

"I don't need to prepare, but I want to have a look into something," Mutana replied, grabbing Irabella's arm and guiding her through the crowd quicker.

"Look into what?"

"Remember those guys that tried kidnapping you? They said the guy that paid them was in Orkestra. I want to try to find him."

Irabella was confused,

"Why would you want to find him?"

"Because we don't know what he was after. I don't even think he was after us. I think he wanted another sorceress and I want to find out who and why."

They had made their way to the front of the crowd and Mutana let go of Irabella's arm and they stopped on the side of the road.

"Okay, I wanna help. Where do we start?"

Mutana smiled and they began walking again.

"I know of a Fallidox who lives in the Housing District. He's shady, but he might be able to help us," Mutana explained as they walked to the gate into the Market District.

They made their way through the gate and the streets were overcrowded, full of kids playing, and street performers, but Mutana and Irabella paid no attention to the fake mages who performed in the street for gold pieces. They saw them as insults, pretending to be mages and not using their skills for good but only profit. It made Irabella angry just seeing how many children were obsessed with these tricks. One of the street performers noticed Mutana and Irabella wearing their mage robes and called them. It was an Elf with yellow skin, pitch black hair and thick eyebrows.

"Come now ladies, why not show us what you can do," he shouted as they walked past. Mutana scoffed at the idea of comparing herself to him and they continued walking. Before they could walk too far, a small dragon made of fire flew in front of Mutana's face and spun into a shower of embers. Mutana stopped walking.

"Now it's your turn, oh noble sorceress," the Elf said, bowing sarcastically. Without a word Mutana spun around, placing two fingers slightly spaced apart over her mouth and blew. A twenty-foot dragon made of raging fire emerged from her mouth, moving through the air like a snake towards the Elf. He froze in his place as the dragon's mouth opened and then disappeared just before it reached him, although the heat alone was enough to sear his eyebrows off. The Elf, still paralyzed with fear, stood still and Mutana smiled. She continued walking and everyone on the street who had stopped to watch were now clapping as they walked away.

"The title of mage has to be earned," Irabella mumbled under her breath. They made their way to the Housing District. Mutana paused for a moment and looked down each direction of the street.

"What's wrong?" Irabella asked.

"I've never been here in person and I can't remember where it is," Mutana responded, squinting her eyes and looking back and forth.

"Should we ask someone?" Irabella asked.

"No this guy is... well, he's a criminal. He loans money, off the book bets and hired muscle. He's not the kinda guy that wants to be easily found."

"So, how do you know about him?" Irabella asked with a judgemental voice.

"I helped arrest a thief once who told us he worked for him. We sent word to guards here, but the last I heard he had most of the guards in his pocket."

Irabella was still confused and suspicious of how Mutana knew where he was, but they both had dark pasts, so she chose not to keep asking questions. Eventually they decided on a direction and began walking. They made their way through the jungle of houses and Irabella looked up and saw some beautiful purple lilies. They were her favourite, and this small thing made her day.

"That's it!" Mutana shouted, pointing at the flowers. "The house with the flowers in the window!" She quietly said enthusiastically.

"Do we knock?" Irabella asked looking at the rotting front door.

"Worth a try," Mutana responded by knocking on the door. A few minutes later, an old lady answered.

With a sweet, soft voice she asked, "What can I do for you?"

Mutana and Irabella looked at each other, confused, and then Mutana shrugged and said, "We are looking for Sam."

The old lady smiled and waved them inside. They walked inside the strangely empty house; nothing more than a fire in the corner and a pot boiling above it. The old lady shuffled to the back room and they followed. She stopped and knocked on the wall, suddenly the wall panel shifted back and slid to one side.

"Down there, my dear," the old lady said smiling.

Irabella began to get nervous as they made their way down a creaking staircase into the hidden basement. It was a dark basement with nothing but a single candle sitting on a desk with papers and coins scattered all over it. Behind the desk was an orange furred Falidox. He was wearing a long back cloak with his hood up but stopping at his pointed ears, the bottom half of his face was covered in snow white fur like a beard and flowing down his neck and chest behind his string tied shirt. Sam spoke in a low and gravelly voice.

"Why would two mages be knocking at my door, and a tournament participant no less?"

"I want to ask you about something," Mutana replied, smiling, wanting to be polite.

"And what could that be, I wonder?" Sam said, smiling back.

"We have learnt that there is a man here in Orkestra who has placed a bounty on a sorceress. We don't know who or why but we are trying to track the man down. Women are being attacked on the streets and we need to know if you have any part of it."

Sam took his feet off of his desk and walked around to face Mutana. His yellow eyes were piercing and this put her on edge.

“Let me assure you, my men have very strict rules about harming women. I don't care about the money or what they have done, no women are harmed from my business ventures.” He paused and looked at Irabella. “Fallidox... Human... or Gormen - do I make myself clear?” He looked back at Mutana as he said this.

“Of course, Sam. I didn’t mean to offend you. I only meant has he asked you for help or have any of your employees heard anything about it?” Mutana replied, her heart beating faster and faster. His body language changed immediately, and he began smiling again.

"Oh good. I don't want you ladies getting the wrong idea about me. But, to answer your question, yes. A stranger approached me a week ago and asked if I could spare any men to help his search. He offered me a large sum of gold for it as well. But, I told him what I told you - although he didn't take it as well as you did and my boys here had to escort him out." He waved his hand gesturing at the two large men sitting in the corner of the room that Irabella hadn't even noticed until that moment.

"What did he look like?" Mutana asked.

"Couldn't tell you to be honest. He had a large hood on and a scarf covering his face, but I could tell by the smell it was a Gormen, but not your kind. He was a pact Goblin."

"A pact Goblin?" Irabella interjected.

"Pact Goblins are savages who live out in the wild, they are barbarians, blood thirsty and violent. They make clans with the blood Elves who share the same kind of nature," Mutana replied.

"Okay, so where can we find him?" Irabella said, impatient for answers. Sam's eyes drifted over to her and smiled.

"A long way from here I assure you. My boys made sure he was on a horse and he's probably halfway to Tortu by now."

"Great, so we will never find him," Irabella said, frustrated.

“This is good Irabella - a pact Goblin in the city would have been extremely dangerous. It's lucky he's gone, I just wish we could have found out why he was searching for sorceresses,” Mutana said, placing her hand on Irabella's shoulder. “But it's over, the city is a little safer now.”

“He did tell me the name of the witch he was looking for,” Sam said, walking back over to his chair. Mutana and Irabella both looked at him, waiting for the name. “Sireana Silvertongue, the most wanted woman in Concorvia right now.”

This surprised Mutana. Irabella was aware of Sireana, but only knew what the wanted posters said about her.

“Why would a savage want to find Sireana Silvertongue?” Irabella asked. “Do they even need gold? What would they do with the bounty?”

“I don't know, but it can't be good,” Mutana replied. “Thank you for your time Sam and thank you for your help. We will show ourselves out.” Sam bowed his head slightly and Mutana and Irabella left the basement. They exited the house and Mutana was deep in thought.

“What does this mean?” Irabella asked.

“I don't know, none of it makes sense. pact Goblins never leave their tribes apart from hunting and war. Coming to a large city to search for criminals is unheard of.” Mutana paused for a moment, deep in thought once again. “I need to complete some errands to prepare for tomorrow. I'll meet you back at the George later tonight and maybe you should try to find Jariko and Kellarom as well."

"But I thought you didn't have to prepare for tomorrow? Plus, you disappeared last night for a few hours as well, what do you have to do alone?" Irabella asked. Mutana was acting strange, and she didn't know why.

"Don't worry about it Bella, I'll see you later."

And just like that Mutana had disappeared into the crowd of people. Something didn't feel right to Irabella so she decided to follow Mutana; she wanted to help. She lost sight of her for a while before she found her passing through the gate into the Grand District. Irabella followed Mutana down the road for a short distance before they reached the colosseum and Mutana entered. It was then that Irabella thought about what was happening. Mutana was just going to train in the colosseum.

All the strange stuff going on, the tournament, Moritus, the pact Goblin, and now the criminal Sireana who could be in the city. This was all too overwhelming for her. Irabella decided to let Mutana train in peace and let off some steam to prepare for tomorrow. Irabella went to the Market District before going back to the inn. She hoped she would bump into Jariko and Kellarom if she walked around long enough.

Chapter Nineteen: The Investigation

After their talk with the Grandmaster, Kellarom had already left the Cosilica by the time Jariko had started making his way down the long staircase. He found himself in the main hall that he'd visited the day before. The strange statue still lingered at the end of the room. Jariko stared at it for a moment but tore himself away and continued to the main door. Kellarom was squatting against the wall breathing heavily. He looked up at Jariko.

"I'm going after her, you can't stop me Jariko."

"I wanna help, Moritus was my friend and I wanna get justice for him too."

Kellarom's eyes lit up and a smile grew on his face.

"Thanks," Kellarom said before standing up and walking over to Jariko.

"So what's the plan?" Jariko asked.

"We need to find out where people place bets."

"But there must be dozens of places people go to place bets. We need to find one that a criminal would be comfortable going to." Kellarom placed both hands on the back of his head and closed his eyes. "How are we gonna find something like that without raising suspicions?" Kellarom asked.

"We could ask the guards?" Jariko suggested.

"They will just think we're criminals ourselves and arrest us," Kellarom replied, hopelessness in his voice.

"I could ask Gregarous! He's that young guard who dragged me away yesterday. I'm sure he might have an idea where criminal stuff like betting goes on," Jariko exclaimed.

"It's the best idea we have so far - let's do it. Where can we find him?" Kellarom asked.

"I last saw him in the Market District, outside Commander Claypius' office. We should start there."

Without hesitation, the two boys began running again down the path towards the gate to the Market District, however, further down the path was blocked by hundreds of people trying to get back into the lower districts. They were all the spectators from the colosseum.

"I really don't feel like trying to get through all those people," Kellarom said, breathing heavily and looking nervous. Then, Jariko remembered that the inner walls were hollow, and he came up with a plan.

"If we can find a door that leads inside the wall, maybe we can sneak through as a shortcut. Avoid the gate all together."

Kellarom nodded and they darted off the path and around the crowd of people until they reached the wall that separated the Grand District and the Market District.

"Where is the door to the inside?" Kellarom asked curiously.

"I dunno - the only one I used was in the gate arch, but there have to be others," Jariko replied. They made their way along the edge of the wall, avoiding being seen by any farmers or guards.

They walked for thirty minutes before Jariko saw something up ahead.

"A door!" He shouted. They sprinted the rest of the way and arrived at the decrepit door.

"It doesn't look like it's been used in centuries," Kellarom said doubtfully. Jariko tried the handle, but it was locked.

"What a surprise," Kellarom said sarcastically. "Let me have a go," he added while walking up to the door. Kellarom placed his finger over the keyhole and a strange light began emitting from his finger.

"I can fill the keyhole with my magic, then make the shape of the key and…" he turned his finger, and they heard the graceful sound of the lock clicking open. Kellarom slowly pushed the door open and looked inside.

"It's a long corridor," he whispered quietly. "I can't see anyone."

He slowly made his way inside. Jariko took a final look around to make sure no one was watching and followed him.

Jariko closed the door behind them. They found themselves in a dark corridor. It seemed to run endlessly in either direction and it was too dark to see any details. The only light available were thin beams of light through the wood cracks. Every beam of light had dust passing through it like a waterfall and it made it unpleasant to breathe.

"Let's hurry; I don't like the dark," Jariko explained thinking back to the Roach-lin tunnels. They decided to head left, looking for any door to the other side.

Jariko ran his hands along the wall as they walked, hoping to feel the edge of a door but he never found one.

Eventually they found themselves at the end of the corridor with a large door blocking the way. Once again Kellarom got the door open and they were pleasantly surprised to see torches lighting the way for them, so they continued down the corridor. It began to get more crowded with piles of bags, boxes and barrels.

"These must be the supplies for the guards," Kellarom pointed out, opening a box to see that it was full of arrows. They knew that this must be a busier part of the wall and they'd have a high chance of getting caught so they didn't stick around. However, they began to hear faint footsteps heading towards them.

"Hide!" Kellarom whispered in a panic.

They rushed around trying to find somewhere before Jariko found two empty barrels.

"Kell, in here! Quick!"

The two climbed into the barrels and waited for the footsteps to pass. They knew that if they got caught the guards would think they were robbers, or worse, enemy spies, and they didn't want to know what happened to spies. The footsteps grew louder and Jariko's heart began racing, he tried to calm himself down but then he heard a voice.

It was the guard that was walking towards them; he was talking to himself.

"Must get the supplies quick, then clean the horses and string the bows. Can't forget about dinner, then polish all the swords..." he continued talking faster and with an endless list of things to do. It was a squeaky voice, but Jariko recognised it - he peeked his head out slightly from the barrel to see that it was Gregarous.

"Gregarous!" Jariko shouted while jumping out of the barrel. Gregarous screamed so loud it left a ringing in Jariko's ears.

"You again!?" Gregarous shouted trying to catch his breath.

Jariko climbed out of the barrel and then knocked the barrel Kellarom was hiding in and Kellarom began to climb out as well.

"Who's this? What are you doing in here?" Gregarous shouted with a sense of nervousness.

"We were looking for you, Gregarous. I told my friend about you and he was dying to meet you!" Jariko said trying to pretend they planned it, hoping Gregarous wouldn't immediately go running to a guard.

"Me?! Why would we want to meet me?" Gregarous replied, confused.

"Kellarom didn't believe me when I told him I made a friend who was a guard."

Kellarom realised what Jariko was trying to do.

"This kid isn't a guard, he's just the cleaner," Kellarom stated in a cocky voice.

"I am a guard!" Gregarous said trying to stand tall.

"See!" Jariko said putting his arm around Gregarous.

"I bet he doesn't know anything about any criminals."

"I do so," Gregarous replied sounding slightly upset.

"Okay then, where do criminals go to bet on stuff?" Kellarom asked, Jariko worried no one would be stupid enough to fall for this plan.

"Actually, I heard Commander Claypius talking about a man called Shady Sam. He runs an illegal betting house out of one of the flats in the Housing District. Is that criminal enough for you?" Gregarous said, clearly instantly regretting it, but trying to pretend like he didn't care. Jariko and Kellarom were surprised - their terrible plan had worked.

"Wow, you really are a protector of the city. I'm sorry for doubting you," Kellarom said. Gregarous was confused but a cocky smile grew on his face.

“Thanks, Gregarous. Oh and before you go - is there a door through to the Market District near here?” Jariko asked politely.

“Yeah, follow me,” Gregarous replied puffing out his chest. He walked them down to a locked door, got out his keys and opened the door for them.

“Wait why were you in the…” Gregarous tried to ask but Jariko interrupted him.

“I'll see you round Gregarous!” Jariko shouted while he and Kellarom waved goodbye. Gregarous waved back, still confused while he closed the door behind them.

"I can't believe that worked," Kellarom whispered to Jariko.

They both chuckled at the ridiculousness of their plan. Jariko was happy that he could distract Kellarom enough to see him smile, but it only worked for a while. A few minutes later Jariko could see that Kellarom was thinking about his brother.

They made their way through the Market District. Distraught and not wanting to draw too much attention, Kellarom walked with his head down. Jariko wanted to talk to him but he didn't know what to say, so instead they walked in silence.

Jariko tried to take note of everything he saw as they walked through the amazing city. The sound of smashing metal as a Tunere blacksmith hammered away, embers from the fire falling on his large shell then simmering out of existence; two Goblin children and a Falidox cub chased a Human boy through the streets, laughing and playing; even an Elf street performer making small dragons out of fire that would fly up into the sky and then explode. Although, he did seem on edge and his eyebrows were missing, maybe by a spell gone wrong. Nevertheless, Jariko was entranced by the life in the city. He promised himself he would live here one day.

After making their way to the Housing District they stopped.

"So, what now?" Kellarom asked, looking at the large number of houses. "Knock on every door and ask for a known criminal?" He added sarcastically.

Jariko stood in silence thinking. There had to be an easy way to find Shady Sam. Then, Jariko saw an old Orc beggar sitting on the floor in ragged clothes and a tattered hat sat in front of him on the ground. Jariko thought nothing of him at first, just like every other person walking past without giving him a second look but this gave Jariko an idea. He walked up to the old Orc.

"I'm looking for someone," Jariko said to the Orc. He slowly looked up at Jariko, squinting his eyes.

"Everybody's looking for som'in," the Orc replied in a gravelly voice. "Why dontcha be more specific."

"Me and my friend are looking for someone who could lend us gold. We were told to find Shady Sam."

The old Orc's pointed ears pricked up.

"Shady Sam, ah, I think I've ‘eard that name before. Would be easier to remember wiv some gold in me hand." He raised his hat into the air and shook it at Jariko.

"We don't have any gold. He just told you, we are looking for someone to give us some," Kellarom snapped back at the old Orc.

"Then I don't remember Shady Sam," the Orc replied, placing his hat back down on the muddy ground.

"What about some food?" Jariko asked, reaching into his bag, pulling out some bread and cheese he was saving for later.

"That'll do nicely. Creators bless you."

No one said anything for a few moments as the Orc tore off a piece of bread.

"Well?!" Kellarom snapped again.

"Oh yes, my old mind ent what it used to be. I dunno where Shady Sam is, but I see a lot of shady looking people hanging around a ‘ouse not ‘undred paces from ‘ere. Look for the top ‘ouse wiv purple flowers in the window. The crack between the ‘ouses is where they like to meet. Can't tell you who or when, that's all I know." The old Orc began eating his bread once again.

"Thank you," Jariko said smiling. They started walking in the direction the old beggar pointed them in.

"Damn Orcs, I hate them," Kellarom mumbled. "Always want everything from you."

He clenched his fists in anger. Jariko thought it best he didn't ask about it and they continued walking.

They found the house with the purple flowers in the window, a hundred paces from the beggar just like he said. They were purple lilies. Jariko always liked lilies, they reminded him of his mother, however, these looked like they had not been watered for a few days. Such beauty within a cramped, grey place warmed Jariko's heart. They decided to sit on some stairs a few houses down to not draw any attention and waited.

The sun was beginning to set, and it had been a long day. Jariko could tell that Kellarom was struggling. He hadn't had the time to properly grieve. He was in denial about what had happened, and he didn't want to accept it, pretending like it never happened but still having small moments of sadness and disbelief. It seemed like it was really taking hold of him now; he hadn't spoken more than a few words for a while and wouldn't stop looking at the floor. This investigation was all he had to keep his mind off of his brother, but what about when it was over, and it was time to accept what happened? Jariko had no idea what to do or what to say to make it better. Then he realised that nothing would. Kellarom had lost his brother. That was a scar that he would have to live with for the rest of his life. During this train of thought Jariko was interrupted by Kellarom.

"Look," he whispered. There were two men in long coats and their faces hidden by their hoods. They looked around and straight at Jariko and Kellarom. They darted their eyes down to the ground to not spook the strange men. Once satisfied, the two men walked into the alley between the house. Jariko and Kellarom quickly stood up and followed. Jariko peeked around the corner. They were gone. Confused, Jariko and Kellarom walked down the alley and they stood there in the empty void for a moment trying to figure out where the men could have gone. But then Kellarom noticed something behind an old wagon. It was a trap door leading to the basement of the house. They pushed the wagon forward, and then let it go so that it rolled back down to its original spot.

"That's how they disappear so quickly - they push the wagon and before it rolls back, they climb inside and it hides the entrance," Jariko stated in disbelief of their ingenuity.

"I wonder what people like this could accomplish if they weren't criminals," Kellarom added, helping Jariko push the wagon back up and quickly but quietly opening the trap door and they both climbed inside. However, they soon realised that they were now trapped with the criminals.

They found themselves in a dark room. It smelt damp and was filled with wooden boxes covered in thick dust. They could hear voices from around the corner and saw a light flickering. Slowly creeping towards the light, Jariko pulled his axe from his back ready, when suddenly they were grabbed from behind. Jariko's axe was torn from his hand and a strong muscular arm wrapped itself around his throat. They were dragged to the faint light. A small candle flickered on a desk covered in paper and gold pieces. Sat at the desk was a Falidox who Jariko could only assume was Shady Sam. He hadn't met a fully grown Falidox before, especially a criminal. The face of the beast man with his yellow eyes and sharp teeth intimidated Jariko and he was even more on edge when Sam spoke.

“I really am popular today, another Human and Goblin duo? What can I do for you two? Did that stupid Gormen send you?” Jariko and Kellarom looked at each other confused.

“We… don't know what you’re …talking about…” Jariko said, struggling to get his words out from the hold around his neck.

“So, if you're not here to bother me then why are you here?” Sam replied.

“We wanted... to ask you... something,” Kellarom said, also struggling. Sam leant forward in his chair and raised his hand and the two men let go of Jariko and Kellarom. The men walked over to stand next to Sam - it was the men they had followed in.

“Ask me what?” Sam asked, beginning to sound impatient.

“Who has had the largest bet placed on them?” Jariko asked, rubbing his neck.

“Why would you wan…” Sam asked, pausing to add, “Aren't you that Goblin mage’s brother? The one who died this morning?” Sam pointed at Kellarom. Kellarom’s face dropped but he held back any emotions he was experiencing.

“That's why we are here. He was murdered and we think we can help find the person who did it!” Jariko took a step while talking and Sam's bodyguards stepped forward too before Sam stopped them. “We think someone is rigging the matches, most likely to win a bet placed with you.”

Sam paused, then stood up and walked around his desk to stand in front of Kellarom.

"I put all my money on your brother winning, a large amount of money and I lost that today. If someone cheated me, then I want them dead just as much as you," Sam said. Kellarom raised his head to look at Sam. His eyes were welling with tears but he refused to cry. Sam turned to his men and nodded. A man walked over to a large safe in the corner and unlocked it, pulling out a large book.

"If answering a simple question like that will help find and kill them, then I'll help you. Just this once," Sam said walking back over to his desk. He opened the book and it had hundreds of names and numbers covering every inch of the pages.

"All my bets are anonymous. People leave the money and bets in dead drops around the city and my boys here pick it up, so I can't tell you who, but my largest bet placed is on... the Goblin Mutana, five thousand gold."

As strange as it was, Jariko kept himself calm. He was worried Mutana would be in danger, but he realised if Sireana wanted Mutana to win, she couldn't be safer.

"That is weird though," Sam added going over more pages for the tournament.

"What?" Jariko asked.

"Mutana had no sponsors or any achievements to her name. She has the lowest odds to win and this is the only bet I know of that's been placed on her. That's with every booky in the city, even the legal ones," Sam said closing the book.

"That must be why they picked Mutana - to get the largest pay out available," Kellarom said, clearing his throat as he spoke.

"Well, I've told you what you wanna know, now get out, and if you mention this place or even speak my name, I'll have you killed and fed to a feral Shatorem. Those shark people are gruesome."

Even though he knew Sam was kidding, or at least he hoped he was, it still scared Jariko so he nodded and turned to leave, picking his axe up from the floor and putting it on his back.

Just as Kellarom was about to leave the room Sam spoke up again.

"Hey kid, I'm sorry about your brother," Sam smiled as he said this, revealing his rows of sharp teeth. Kellarom smiled back politely. They walked to the hatch where they'd entered, then one of the men walked over and pulled on a large rope hanging above them. They opened the hatch, and the wagon wasn't in the way. Once they had climbed out, the door closed behind them and the wagon rolled back into place hiding the door perfectly.

It was dark now and the street was basically empty, but they were safe. The two young men looked at each other and smiled, then laughed and hugged. Kellarom couldn't help but start crying into Jariko's shoulder. They had been through a lot and both of them were scared.

They decided not to tell Mutana or Irabella what they had learnt, to spare them the stress and fear, but they were satisfied that they were a step closer in finding justice for Moritus.

"Come stay with us at the George," Jariko said. "We can find Sireana tomorrow after the second challenge of the tournament. We might find some clues or stop something bad from happening."

Kellarom nodded and they headed to the inn for some food and rest. It had been a very long day.

Chapter Twenty: The Tournament Continues

After meeting Irabella at the inn, the three young adventurers had a quiet meal together. None of them wanted to discuss what had happened or what they'd found that day, trying to spare each other the danger they could be in.

Eventually they grew tired. Kellarom stayed in Jariko's room and Irabella retired to her room. Mutana did not return to the inn until much later that night. Irabella was laying in her bed pretending to be asleep, but she couldn't sleep alone. She had to have someone with her - it was just another habit she'd picked up from sleeping on the streets. She didn't want to bother Mutana; she could tell she'd had a long night of training so she decided to stay in bed and let Mutana rest.

The next morning, the four met downstairs and began eating breakfast. Kellarom hadn't said a word since last night and none of the others wanted to talk about the previous day. Instead, they all ate in silence and when the time came to head out, they all started getting ready, apart from Jariko. He was already fully dressed and with his poncho on since he came down for breakfast.

"Do you ever take that old rag off?!" Irabella said in disgust.

"He slept in it too," Kellarom added under his breath, almost as if he didn't mean for people to hear it. Jariko gave him a look of betrayal and Kellarom shrugged.

"That's so disgusting!" Irabella cried.

"You haven't taken it off once in the past week since we've been traveling together?!" Mutana said, surprised.

"My mother told me to never take it off when I'm not at home; it protects me," Jariko said, trying to defend himself.

“Why don't you just take it off?” Irabella said, reaching to lift his poncho up.

Jariko recoiled away from her hand. He was embarrassed and didn't want to talk about it anymore.

“Fine, if you wanna wear it that much then fine,” Irabella raised her hands in defeat.

"Sorry, Jariko. If you don't want to take it off, don't feel bad," Mutana added, placing her hand on his shoulder, smiling. It was obvious there was a reason he didn't want to take it off so Irabella felt bad for pushing him, but she didn't want to apologise. They stood there for a moment awkwardly before Kellarom walked to the door and left. They looked at each other and followed. Jariko ran to catch up with Kellarom and the group made their way to the colosseum. Jariko and Kellarom began talking about what they'd learnt the day before.

"So, what's the plan?" Kellarom asked, beginning to become livelier.

"We need to try and keep our eyes open for anything strange - anyone acting suspicious or people going to places where they shouldn't," Jariko explained, making it up as he spoke. He had no idea what they should do next but he wanted to give Kellarom hope. He had no idea if they would get any further with the investigation.

They soldiered on to the colosseum for the second day of the tournament. Hundreds of people were swarming into the Grand District wanting to get the best seats. However, Mutana was allowed to skip the crowd and the other three followed her through the gap of people right to the main entrance. They entered the colosseum and Mutana said her goodbyes as she headed to a different section to wait for her next event. Just like the day before, they decided to head near the top so they could get a better view into the arena. They were luckily given a table by a lovely couple who had to leave suddenly so Jariko, Irabella and Kellarom took a seat and waited for the event to start, they were all nervous beyond words and Jariko's heart wouldn't stop racing.

"What if I have to jump into the arena with all these people watching? What if I have to battle Sireana, what if I get it wrong and attack the wrong person? What if I miss something and don't do anything?" Jariko kept asking himself these questions, and his mind was running so quickly that he found himself in a panic until Irabella, who was sitting next to him, put her hand on his shoulder.

"Are you okay Jariko?" She asked softly; it wasn't the normal way she spoke. She sounded genuinely worried about him. Jariko instantly felt better. His mind slowed down and his heart started beating normally.

"I'm fine, just worried about Mutana," he replied, smiling, not actually lying but not wanting to explain everything to keep her safe. Irabella smiled back.

"Yeah, me too."

She didn't want to tell Jariko anything either. Kellarom had barely spoken since they left the inn and Jariko didn't know what to do that would help. He decided to not try anything and let Kellarom grieve in his own way.

They were sitting at their table for twenty minutes and the tournament had not begun. They started to spend time discussing what they were going to do after this week was over. Kellarom decided to join in and tell them that he and his brother had planned to travel the world and become the greatest mages, learn every class of magic and someday unlock Pure magic and have stories told about them. He wanted to keep this dream alive in his brother's memory. Moritus had always said Kellarom was destined for greatness but right now he was only slightly above average.

Jariko told them about his plan to travel around and try to find his father. He had left him and his mother when he was born and left them with nothing. He had no idea where to start looking or what he would do if he found his father but Jariko had no intention of heading home. Irabella was the only one who had no idea what she wanted to do. Mutana would be Grandmaster and she wouldn't want to go home alone.

"Maybe we should all travel together!" Jariko said excitedly. Kellarom sprung up and got excited at this idea too, but Irabella wasn't too fond of it. The two boys looked at her smiling before they shook hands. As they were discussing this new idea, the Grandmaster stepped out and began addressing the audience.

"Hello good people of Concorvia, welcome back. Unfortunately, Sheladon has not been seen today and won't be able to host today's event. So, for today, I shall be stepping in for him to introduce the next challenge for the remaining contestants."

Something seemed off with the Grandmaster; Jariko could tell something was wrong.

"Can the remaining four contestants please enter the arena," Merlon shouted and waved his hands at the door as the remaining mages entered. Mutana was joined by three male mages and the four made a line in the centre of the arena. The Grandmaster smiled and turned back to the crowd.

"Yesterday, we wanted to test out the mages battle prowess. Today, we want to test their bravery." He paused for dramatic effect before raising his hand to hold up four fingers.

"Four buildings have been ignited into a blaze around the city and four helpless victims lay inside. You have one hour to find one of the buildings and carry your victim back here for medical attention." As he explained this, four loud explosions erupted all around the city. The crowd were shocked but then began to cheer uncontrollably.

"Begin!" Merlon shouted and the four mages darted to the exits. Most of the crowd decided to follow them, charging down the stairways and running at full speed so they didn't miss anything. They wanted to see the mages in action but Jariko didn't want to lose his seat and neither did Kellarom or Irabella.

"I would prefer to see who wins," Irabella commented. Jariko and Kellarom nodded in agreement.

"Why have they picked this for a challenge?" Jariko asked, disappointed he wouldn't be able to watch it in its entirety.

"It's a hard thing to do when you think about it. Each mage has to find a fire, get to the location and save someone from the fire without getting injured, plus because it's a race. They have to think quickly on their feet - should they go to the closest fire and risk losing the victim to someone else or go straight to a fire that's further away and have to travel a lot further?" Irabella explained.

"It's gonna take a lot of planning and they're gonna have to use every trick they have to get back here first," Kellarom added. Jariko pretended to understand.

"So, what is it testing?" Jariko asked.

"I guess their decision making in an emergency situation," Irabella replied, scratching her head. As they were talking a mage walked into the arena. He was a human man, bald with strange symbols all over his head and he was wearing strange red robes.

"That's a Videre monk!" Kellarom shouted standing up to get a better look.

"What's a Videre monk?" Jariko asked.

"The Videre are ancient people who give up their own sight and see through the eyes of the universe - or so they say," Irabella explained, scoffing at the notion.

"It's all true - they could see anywhere in the universe if they wanted to. I knew Concorvia had one but I never thought I would get to see him," Kellarom replied excitedly. It was the first time he had properly smiled that day.

“The monks who choose to live in civilisation are mainly used for military tactics and strategic planning by the city guards,” Kellarom explained further.

"You mean they can see everything all the time?!" Jariko replied, astonished.

"No one really knows. No one knows how they get the powers or even the limits of them. The monks don't tell anyone outside their temples," Irabella said. This power seemed amazing to Jariko. He had never heard of such a thing and was determined to find out one day, but for now they still had to find out why one of these monks was at the tournament.

Before Jariko could ask why they thought he might be there the monk stepped to the centre of the arena and kneeled down and with a thunderous voice he began to speak.

"The participants have reached the Market Districts where the first fire is located. Two have entered the building while one has continued running and the fourth has also continued but in a different direction," the monk announced.

"Oh, I see, so for the people who don't wanna run after the mages, they have an announcer to commentate over what's happening," Irabella was clearly impressed with the preparation.

"But which one is which? Did Mutana go into the first house, or did she keep running?" Jariko asked excitedly.

"I don't know, maybe there's a limit to their power," replied Irabella while taking out her notebook to write notes in it.

"The other two participants have reached the other houses. The first participant to save a hostage is returning to the colosseum, however, the other participant still hasn't left the first house," the monk continued to commentate.

"If they have already saved the hostage what's the other mage still doing in the burning house?" Kellarom shouted. The monk didn't reply, he just continued giving more details of the contest.

"What if they fought?" Jariko asked.

Kellarom turned around, replying, "Unlikely - if they kill someone outside of the first fighting contest then they will be disqualified. They probably just got stuck or passed out."

"Isn't someone gonna save them?!" Jariko asked. Before Kellarom could respond the first participant returned with his victim on his shoulders. The crowd exploded with applause as Paralom entered the arena, but Kellarom was no longer excited when he saw it was the Elf that had killed Moritus. Kellaroms smile quickly disappeared, the memory of their fight replaying in his mind.

But he knew this wasn't the person he should point his anger at. He turned to Jariko. "I wonder where Mutana is then?"

Jariko could hear the cracking of Kellarom's voice. He was holding back tears. He obviously wanted to think of other things to take his mind off of his brother.

"I dunno. Hopefully she's at least second," Jariko replied.

“Shhhh…” Irabella said to both the boys as the monk was beginning to speak.

“The second and third participants have saved their victims and are on their way back to the Colosseum. One is running north and another south at high speeds both carrying their vic…”

He stopped speaking for a second then continued.

“One of the contestants has collapsed; they could not take the weight. The other participant is running without slowing and is now in the Grand District once again.”

Irabella began to sweat, praying to her Creator that it wasn't Mutana that had fallen.

“The participant is desperately trying to lift their victim back onto their shoulders… it doesn't loo…” he stopped again before continuing. “There seems to be a problem with the first contestant. They are still trapped in the burning house and this participant has gone to help, giving up on the race completely.”

“Something must have gone really wrong in the first house,” Irabella pointed out to Jariko before turning her head to see Toralium, the powerful human mage, enter the arena with his victim. Irabella's face dropped in fear, Jariko turned to her.

“So, which one is Mutana!?” he exclaimed

Jariko bit his lip anxiously as they all waited for the next update.

“The participant has entered the first burning building in order to save the other participant!” He didn't say anything for a few minutes.

“Both participants have left the house just as it collapsed behind them!” the monk exclaimed, getting a little excited himself and the crowd exploded in applause once again, the monk then continued. “Although, it seems they are both now unconscious and are being seen by medics.” Before the monk had finished speaking Irabella ran out, running down the stairs to find Mutana, Jariko and Kellarom looked at each other before jumping up and chasing after her.

Chapter Twenty-One: Sireana Silvertongue

The three of them ran through the Grand District darting in between the crowds of people. Some were leaving to see the aftermath and others were returning to see the closing ceremony for the winners. Jariko and his friends didn't care; only two contestants could go onto the final competition and Mutana had already lost, but they didn't have time to grieve over her defeat, they weren't even sure if she was still alive.

As they were approaching the gate in the wall, they saw a large crowd of people surrounding the smouldering pile of ash which was the burning house. The crowds were flooding into the Grand District completely blocking the gate like hundreds of ants trying to fit through a crack in a rock. Within moments of getting to the gate Jariko had already lost sight of his friends. He began pushing his way through. His height and natural clumsiness made it a challenge to reach the other side, falling over and stepping on people's toes. He eventually made his way through the crowd and fell into the opening onto his hands and knees. He looked up and saw Kellarom. He ran over and helped Jariko to his feet. Jariko smiled at Kellarom before his attention was caught by the sight of Irabella huddled over Mutana's body.

"Is she…" Jariko asked, choking on the words.

"She's fine, just unconscious. The medic said it was lucky she's a pyromancer otherwise the fire would have killed her," Kellarom said, putting his hands on his hips.

"What about the other mage? I don't see another body."

"They have already taken him. He wasn't as lucky, but they said he should survive thanks to Mutana. Apparently, there was a problem and the mage who was supposed to be here in case of emergencies never showed up," Kellarom said, his voice becoming serious.

"Do you think Sireana made this happen?" Jariko whispered, not wanting the crowd or Irabella to hear.

"Maybe, but it almost backfired - she could have killed Mutana but instead she only caused her to lose," Kellarom replied, matching the volume of Jariko's voice.

"She obviously underestimated Mutana."

"Maybe not. Maybe she knew that Mutana would have a fighting chance because of her powers."

"And she just didn't expect Mutana to ignore the first house?" Jariko said, slightly overwhelmed.

"That must have been her plan - to give Mutana the advantage in the first house," Kellarom replied, getting visibly angry.

"That doesn't make sense," Jariko said, "There was no way of knowing which house Mutana would have picked, and this is the only one that went wrong." He leant back, putting his hands on his head.

Kellarom crossed his arms in frustration, "Then what was the plan?" Kellarom asked.

"I have no idea."

After a while the crowd began to disperse and Mutana was still unconscious. Jariko carried Mutana back to the George Inn and Irabella sat by her bed waiting for her to wake up. Jariko and Kellarom sat downstairs having something to eat and drink while discussing theories and ideas, trying to figure out a way they could still find Sireana when suddenly the inn doors swung open and they saw a familiar face. The Grandmaster entered the inn, saw Jariko and Kellarom and smiled before walking over to them and taking a seat.

"I had heard your group was staying here, how wonderful to see you again," Merlon said with a large cheerful smile.

"I'm sorry about the other day, Grandmaster," Kellarom said, lowering his head.

"We haven't done anything. We don't know where she is," Jariko added.

"It's okay boys. I'm not here for that, but make sure you stay safe and come and let me know if you do find anything. You know where to find me."

"So, if you're not here for us, why are you here?" Jariko asked. Kellarom was still hanging his head.

"I'm here to see Mutana. I want to make sure she's alright," Merlon smiled as he said this and rubbed the back of Kellarom's head. He lifted his head and smiled back.

"We can take you to her," Kellarom said with a croaky voice.

Jariko looked at his friend with pity but he knew Kellarom wouldn't want to be pitied or reminded further of his brother's death, so Jariko said and did nothing, he just followed Kellarom and the Grandmaster upstairs in silence.

There in Mutana's room they saw Irabella sitting on the same chair where they'd left her over two hours before. She was smiling when she looked over to them with dried tears staining her cheeks and there next to her was Mutana sat up in bed drinking a glass of water.

"You're awake!" Jariko shouted in excitement.

"Yeah, I'm fine. There's no way I would be killed by fire," Mutana replied, placing her glass down on the table. She hadn't noticed the Grandmaster yet, but as soon as he entered the room her back straightened and she began to climb painfully out of bed.

"Don't bother, my darling - you have gone through too much to show me any kind of respectful courtesies," Merlon said, still smiling. Mutana relaxed and leaned back onto her pillow. "What you did today is beyond thanks. You sacrificed your chance of victory to save a fellow mage and that is what this job is all about, putting others before yourself, making hard and selfless decisions to save lives."

"Thank you, Grandmaster," Mutana replied, coughing.

"And that is why I have allowed an extra space for you in the final contest."

The room fell silent. Everyone was in shock. After a few moments the group erupted with excitement. Merlon began laughing cheerfully as they all celebrated.

"Thank you, Grandmaster. I don't know what to say."

"You don't have to say anything, just rest for now. I couldn't extend the competition so make sure you're ready for tomorrow," Merlon said. He walked over to the bed and placed a small bag of tea on the table. "This is my favourite tea, it will make you feel a lot better."

Irabella jumped up and hugged Merlon like a child hugging her grandparents and Mutana began to laugh. Merlon returned the hug and smiled, then after saying his goodbyes he left the room. The group spent the rest of the evening celebrating. Eventually Mutana was able to stand, and they all went downstairs for drinks and food. There was a talented bard playing songs on his lute while singing and dancing around the room. Every song was infectious and every person within the walls couldn't help but sing along and stomp their feet in time with the music. For hours they all danced and sang, there were even large Orc warriors in the inn that night that may have looked scary but after a few drinks were singing along with everyone else.

Jariko had never drunk alcohol before, but Kellarom convinced him to try some mead. He did and was surprised by the sweet and delicious taste. After a few hours every person in the George Inn was so drunk it was like they had all been friends for years. Jariko challenged every warrior to an arm wrestle and beat every single one. This impressed the Orcs so much they accepted Jariko as one of their own, spending the night singing, dancing and even sharing stories with Jariko and Kellarom. Jariko had never had this much fun in his life, but eventually, like every party, it had to end.

Kellarom was passed out on a table spooning an Orc three times the size of him. Irabella was no were to be seen in the sea of unconscious people on the floor and tables so Jariko presumed she must have gone upstairs to bed. However, Jariko wasn't the only one awake - Mutana was sitting at a table in the back of the inn smiling to herself and Jariko joined her.

"How are you still standing? You put back more mead than anyone!" Mutana said genuinely impressed.

"I feel fine. I guess I have a high tolerance for this stuff," Jariko replied holding back a burp. Mutana smiled and laughed.

"There's something special about you," she said. Jariko grinned, blushing at the compliment.

"Why are you still awake? There are only a few hours until sunrise. You need to rest."

"I'm too nervous to sleep. I almost died today. I don't know if I'm ready for tomorrow's challenge," Mutana said, her smile quickly disappearing.

"You'll be fine. You're the most powerful mage in the competition," Jariko replied, holding his smile. Mutana looked at him and smiled back once again.

"Yeah, you're right. All the others are men. Women are always more powerful mages," Mutana said, raising her fist in the air.

"That's the spirit! Besides, just think about how great it will be to call yourself the Grandmaster," Jariko said, taking another sip of his last mead.

"Yeah, you're right, plus, between you and me, I've placed a large bet on myself, so if I do win, I'll be rich enough to buy all of you a house each." Jariko's stomach tightened, and he almost spat out his drink, but he held the shock back, trying to act normal and he continued to talk.

"I thought contestants couldn't bet on themselves," Jariko replied slowly, lowering his cup.

"They can't, but there are people in the city who do anonymous betting. They are a little shifty, but I'm very confident. It's just lucky the Grandmaster let me into the final competition," Mutana said, smiling and sipping from her own drink in disbelief of her luck. Jariko's heart was beating uncontrollably fast, and he couldn't think straight. He barely managed to string a sentence together, but he managed to say.

"How much did you bet?" He asked, sweating, hiding his shaking hands under the table. Mutana leant in, completely oblivious of Jariko's fear.

"Five thousand gold!" Mutana said, smiling as she leant back in her seat. Jariko was desperately trying to stay calm as his mind started to put the pieces together.

"I have to go outside, I think I'm gonna throw up," Jariko spat out after an uncomfortable silence. He stood up and rushed to the door before Mutana could even respond. He barged through the door and took three long deep breaths and tried to calm down.

"A large bet doesn't mean anything," he said to himself. "Maybe we were wrong. Making a large bet doesn't make her Sireana. Sireana might never have even made a bet."

He paced on the muddy street for what felt like hours before deciding he needed more evidence or actual proof, but the idea of Mutana being Sireana was too much, and he couldn't think straight. The more he thought about it, the more it made sense,

No one else would have been able to speak to Moritus before he died except Mutana. She would have been there in the waiting room with him, Jariko thought. His mind was moving too fast, but it was too late to stop.

"She has been wearing that jewelled necklace since the day I met her - what if that's the Artifact?"

And then he had a realisation.

What if she cheated on the exam? Could that be why Sheladon didn't host the tournament today? I need to find Sheladon. And with that final thought Jariko sprinted down the street into the dark moonlit night, praying that he was wrong.

Chapter Twenty-Two: Evidence

Jariko's mind was a blur as he ran through the streets of Orkestra. He could not stop thinking about all the details and trying to think of a way that Mutana couldn't be Sireana, but nothing came. The idea weighed down on him until his absent mind sent his body off course and he fell straight into the mud of the empty city street. Jariko stayed there for a moment on all fours in the mud, holding back tears.

"Why are you crying?" He said to himself. "There's no proof yet, get to Sheladon and then we can deal with it."

He stood back up and carried on running. As he was making his way through the Market District, he heard a low and tired voice yell out to him from the darkness.

“Where are you heading at this time of night, boy?”

Jariko turned around and saw a city guard leaning on the wall of one of the many shops in this area. He was smoking a pipe which lit his face up every time he took a drag from it. His face was aged, and battle worn with a large burn scar on his left cheek and an unkempt ginger beard hung from his chin.

“My dog ran from home sir. I gotta find him by morning or someone will take him.”

Jariko didn't want to lie to the guard, but he couldn't exactly tell the truth. However, in this moment Jariko’s stomach dropped as he realised this guard may recognise him - he had made a name for himself over the past few days, and he might have seen him talking to the Commander. Jariko’s heart raced as the guard looked him up and down in silence for an uncomfortably long amount of time.

“No dogs have run through here, but these streets are dangerous at night boy, you best take care.”

Jariko just nodded and carried on running, not looking back and taking a deep breath as he left the Market District. As Jariko entered the Grand District he stopped as he realised, he had no idea where Sheladon would be.

Is he in the Cosilica or the Colosseum? Or does he live in his own house? Do the mages live in the Cosilica? Is he even a mage?!

Once again, he felt his mind hurtling into a downward spiral. He composed himself and decided to start where he last saw Sheladon; the Colosseum. He had no idea what he was going to do there, but it was too late. He was wet, cold, and too scared to go back. Mutana was probably wondering where he had gone and before he panicked, he tried to brush the idea out of his head.

She probably fell asleep - she won't get suspicious and think you know her secret. She might not even have a secret.

And once again Jariko's mind began swirling once more, but eventually he was at the gate of the Colosseum.

The answers I need have to be in here. The sun will be coming up soon and I need to be back at the inn before then or everyone will get suspicious, especially Kell.

Jariko tried the door and it opened. Was it normal to keep this place unlocked and unguarded?

Jariko hoped he wouldn't bump into a guard who would mistake him for a thief, so he clung to the walls and moved slowly through the dark hallways. He couldn't hear anyone else in the Colosseum and he could see even less; it was too dark to make out details of the areas he was exploring but he didn't want to find a torch in case he had to hide. It was totally dark except for beams of light every ten paces from the full moon outside. This was enough to help Jariko keep his sense of direction and not trip over everything. He found his way to the waiting room that he had been in when he tried to comfort Kellarom after Moritus had died. The air still seemed so heavy with grief but he continued through the halls trying different doors. Some would open but lead to nowhere, and others were locked. He kept trying until one of the last doors opened into a room filled with small tables in rows.

This must be the room they took the exam in, he thought to himself as he began exploring the room. Beams of moonlight shone through the windows illuminating parts of the room. The room wasn't very large. It could only hold nine of these single person tables and one table at the front facing towards the others.

That must be Sheladon's desk, Jariko thought, slowly making his way through the dark room. The desk at the front was larger than the others but only by width. It had three small drawers on either side and each drawer was filled with books, notebooks, sketches and doodles that must have been tied to whatever Sheladon studied and most likely taught. As he was looking through the desk he noticed some soot on the edge of the desk. Jariko looked down at the floor and noticed more where he was standing. He realised that something had been burned. He got onto his knees and stuck his hand under the desk and felt a small pile of burnt papers someone had kicked under the desk. He knew he was getting close.

This must have been Mutana! Burning the evidence.

Jariko quickly realised that if it was Mutana, then the evidence he was looking for had been burnt as well. Defeated, he began to stand back up but as he did, he noticed a folded up piece of paper wedged between the drawers and the tabletop. Jariko gently pulled out the piece of people and unfolded to find it was Mutana's exam sheet.

Sheladon must have known she would try to come back to destroy it! Jariko began to read through the exam. He knew the evidence he needed was somewhere on that sheet of paper.

Question one: If a projectile is thrown at forty yards and travels at a speed of ten metres per second how long will it take for the projectile to hit the target?

Question two: What is the density of a dragon scale?

Question three: What is the temperature of a fire fuelled only with magic?

Question four: How much can an average giant lift and for how long?

Question five: If a nobleman has an army of five thousand and has to travel two hundred miles, how much food will he need to bring to sustain his army for battle?

He couldn't understand the questions or how Mutana had figured out any of the answers but he continued to read all fifty of the questions and answers before coming to the final page. He was amazed how so many of these mages could score high enough to pass this exam and that's when he noticed the evidence he had been searching for this entire time. At the bottom of Mutana's exam it said seventy nine percent - Jariko's heart sank into his stomach.

The pass mark was ninety percent. Why would Sheladon pass Mutana?

He tried to think of reasons of why Mutana might have passed but he knew what the truth was: Mutana was Sireana Silvertongue and had bewitched Sheladon into passing her. His sadness became rage as he had let this woman deceive him all this time, however, it was shortlived as he heard the door opening.

Jariko shoved Mutana's exam into his pocket and stood up. It was a young man dressed in white robes just like Irabella.

"Oh, I'm sorry, can I help you?" The young man asked.

"I...I was looking for Sheladon. I had some questions to ask him about the density of dragon scales," Jariko replied, recalling one of the questions he had read. The young man's face dropped, and his voice became sad as he looked down at the floor.

"I'm afraid Master Sheladon is dead."

Jariko was shocked and sat down on the chair behind him.

"How?!"

"They found him in his home: he hung himself," the young man choked on tears as he spoke.

Jariko didn't know what to say - the man was obviously one of Sheladon's disciples.

"I'm sorry. Was he in some kind of trouble? Was he struggling?" Jariko asked.

"It's strange; Master Sheladon loved his work and never spoke bad about anyone or anything. I guess he just hid it well."

This was the final bit of convincing Jariko needed - Sireana bewitched Sheladon to pass the first exam and made him kill himself just like Moritus. The thought made Jariko want to throw up, but he didn't want this young man asking him any more questions. He could see the sun beginning to rise behind where the man was standing and realized he had to get to the Grandmaster before the tournament started.

"I'm sorry for your loss," Jariko said as he ran out of the room and back down the hallway he had entered from. He threw the door open and was hit by the morning air. There was already a hoard of people making their way to the Colosseum. Jariko knew he had wasted too much time already. He couldn't let the final competition start.

Jariko ran as fast as his legs could carry him, as he barged past countless people, hearing threats and shouts of anger directed towards him. Jariko didn't care. He didn't even take notice that they were there. All he could think of was that one of his closest friends was a cold blooded killer and he had been traveling with her all this time.

He knew he was going to have to confront her soon, very soon, and he also knew he was probably going to have to fight her. This thought scared him the most - he had seen Mutana in battle many times and every time she won leaving her enemies in a pile of smouldering ash on the floor. Jariko was a good fighter, he was strong, and he had his axe, but he knew those things wouldn't be enough. Of course, Kellarom would help him fight, but could he trust Kellarom not to try and kill her?

Does she even deserve to live? Jariko thought, *After all she's done.*

Mutana - no, Sireana - had killed Moritus and Sheladon for no other reason than to become Grandmaster, but she did save that mage yesterday in the fire. Why risk her life to save another participant? It just doesn't make sense... unless she didn't save him because she's a good person, she saved him because she knew she had already lost in the race and saving the man would get her a spot in the final. Maybe that was the plan all along - that's why that house didn't have someone to control the fire. She never intended to win the race.

As Jariko ran, the picture in his mind became more and more clear.

Sireana is a murderer and because of me she made it to the city and made her plan happen. She should have died in that Roach-lin hole and I saved her. I'm just as much to blame as she is, I have to bring her to justice, alive or dead.

Chapter Twenty-Three: Out of Time

As Jariko arrived outside of the Cosilica, the sun was burning bright in the sky. Everyone in the inn would be awake by now. Jariko wandered if Kellarom had noticed he was gone and if he was concerned. Or if Sireana had noticed. It didn't matter as long as he could stop the tournament and then Sireana could be arrested before she even knew what was going on.

The giant doors swung open and Jariko found himself in similar surroundings. The ominous statue stared down at him, the same statue that brings your demons to the surface and the place Jariko had first met the Grandmaster.

He averted his gaze, not wanting to be judged by Agorith and ran to the door that led up to the Grandmaster's library. Jariko struggled up the steps trying not to lose his footing as he made his way up the seemingly endless stairway until he got to the large wooden door. Forcing it open he found himself in the large dusty room that he had been in just the other day and desperately ran around hoping to find the Grandmaster just sitting down reading, but he had no such luck.

After ten minutes of searching this large hall of corridors and areas hidden by shelves of books, he found a ladder hidden away in one of the dark corners of the library. Jariko decided to investigate the ladder, hoping it would lead him to the Grandmaster.

The ladder lead up to a trap door in the ceiling and as he opened the small wooden trap door, it swung back smashing into the concrete floor and the sound echoed up a spiralling staircase. As he climbed up he got an overwhelming sense of claustrophobia and unease.

The older wooden staircase creaked with every step that Jariko took. Time had eaten away at the wood and there didn't seem to be any signs of magical means of repair. This seemed strange considering how breath-taking the rest of the cathedral was. Silky strands of spider webs hung from the bricks filling the chamber with shining strands that glistened in the morning sun, however, Jariko couldn't appreciate the subtle beauty of the webs, they just creeped him out. Although he found it strange that there were this many spider webs in the stairway, it indicated that it wasn't regularly used by the mages. As he pondered this thought, he almost forgot why he was there in the first place and Jariko continued to climb.

Eventually, he found himself standing outside an old wooden door that looked older than Orkestra itself, which it probably was if you believe the Cosilica came before the city. It didn't look like it had been opened for centuries and the rotting wood didn't look secure whatsoever.

Jariko tried the door handle, but the door wouldn't even shake. He tried knocking, but there was no answer. He tried the handle again, but it was sturdier than it looked. It didn't feel like a real door. After a few moments, Jariko decided to kick the door down. He could just say it collapsed by itself. However, even with Jariko's immense strength the door barely shook when his boot met it. Something didn't seem right - a door that appeared to be this flimsy shouldn't be this tough. Then Jariko remembered where he was - the centre for all mages of Concorvia.

The door must be enchanted. Jariko thought, realising that the door would probably never open without a key. He decided to try one last time. Jariko unclipped his axe from his back and readied for a swing. He leant back and threw all of his weight behind the axe into the door. To Jariko's surprise the door exploded into small splinters and shards of wood scattering into the room behind it..

"I didn't think that would work - maybe it wasn't enchanted after all." He put his axe back on his back and entered the room.

The difference from the staircase and the room was night and day. It was quite a large room and seemed to be some kind of laboratory mixed with living quarters. A large bed was tucked into the corner beside a fireplace. Tall bookcases filled with books much older and bigger than the books found downstairs filled the wall opposite the bed and in between was a large round table scattered with strange items, scrolls and tomes.

A chandelier hung from the ceiling above the table, nailed to the wooden beams holding the ceiling up. On the wall opposite from where Jariko was standing was a rectangular glass door that opened out to a moderate balcony. Jariko stepped outside and saw that he was at the top of the Cosilica, the highest place in all of Concorvia and the home to the Grandmaster.

The view was spectacular. Jariko could see all of the Grand District including the Colosseum, the gate leading to the Market District, and he could even see the outer wall and much of the landscape that they had travelled through before they arrived. To his left was the mighty and boundless ocean, Jariko had never seen a sight like it. He was brought back to reality when he noticed the large swarm of people outside the Colosseum. From here they looked like a pulsing mass of ants swarming to the nest, but he knew the tournament would be starting soon and he couldn't be further away. If this was Merlon's home then he had already left and Jariko had no way of getting back down. He realised how much of an idiot he was.

"I should've just stayed at the Colosseum, now people are gonna die!" he told himself, hitting his head in frustration. Then he heard a quiet chirp from inside the room. He turned and saw a small bird sitting on a perch in the corner of the room. He was shocked he hadn't noticed it when he first entered. Jariko recognized the small bird from the storybooks he had read as a child. They were called budgies. They weren't inherently magical but their ability to copy a simple sentence spoken to them by the owner seemed magical; they could then fly off and deliver any message to the person they had been trained to find. The storybooks Jariko owned as a child spoke of Gnomes, tribes of small people who lived in the north that used these birds to send messages in between tribes, groups that were traveling or even use them to scare humans who got too close.

He held out his hand and the small bird jumped onto his finger and chirped once again. The bird had a bright yellow beak and beautiful white colour to its feathers, smaller black feathers in the centre of its wings and its belly had a slightly blue tint. It was truly beautiful and Jariko couldn't help but admire the small bird for a few moments before petting it lightly on its head. The bird closed its eyes as Jariko ran his finger down its back. He was surprised how soft the bird was - he had never touched a bird before.

"Have you got a name, little guy?" Jariko asked, still petting the bird. To his surprise it replied to his question.

"Snowy," the little bird chirped back at him. Jariko recoiled his hand in shock before he smiled and began stroking the bird again.

"That's a pretty name. Do you know where Merlon is?"

"Merlon, Merlon," the bird chirped back.

"Yes, that's it, Merlon. Can you take a message to him for me?"

The bird nodded and Jariko took a deep breath. He didn't want to make it too long otherwise the bird might get it wrong. Jariko cleared his throat and made sure to speak clearly.

"Mutana is Sireana. It's not safe for anyone."

As soon as he had finished speaking the little bird disappeared out of the window and towards the Colosseum. He could hear the quiet roar of the crowds and what sounded like drums beating. It had already started, and he had no idea if he was too late but it was his only chance.

Jariko stood on the balcony watching the Colosseum. He could make out flashes of light and dots darting back and forth from within the Colosseum. The tournament had already started. Just as he was about to belittle himself once again, he felt the ground shake up through the Cosilica to his feet. He saw a flash of light and then an explosion erupt from the Colosseum, decimating the southern wall. A large dust cloud engulfed the structure until it was barely visible. Jariko stumbled backwards to the wall and fell to the ground.

After what felt like the hours, the little bird flew back to Jariko and landed on the railing of the balcony. Jariko got to his feet and the bird spoke. Jariko's hands began shaking, he could feel his heart beating in his throat and he felt like he couldn't breath as the bird continuously repeated the message.

"They're coming, they're coming, they're coming!"

Chapter Twenty-Four: Betrayal

Irabella woke up as soon as the sun hit her face through the window of her room. She noticed Mutana wasn't in the room, so she got dressed and headed downstairs to find her. The first thing she saw when descending the stairs was Kellarom spooning an Orc on a table and the crowd of people still passed out on the floor. Irabella turned her nose up at the sight and gracefully made her way over to Mutana who was asleep on the table at the back.

"Mutana, wake up," she said while shaking her friend. Mutana's head shot up and her eyes began to dart around as she came to consciousness.

"Wow, what happened?" Mutana said, rubbing her eyes.

"It looks like you all drank way too much."

"Yeah, probably. Where's Jariko? I thought he was here with me."

Irabella looked around the room but couldn't find him in the crowd.

"Maybe he went to bed as well," Irabella suggested while walking over to Kellarom. She grabbed a cup of liquid off one of the tables and tipped it over Kellarom's peaceful face. He woke in a panic.

"What's going on?!" He shouted, trying to pull his numb arm out from under the sleeping Orc.

“I hope you two will be very happy together,” Irabella said, gesturing at Kellarom and his new friend.

“I don't remember anything from last night,” Kellarom said standing up and cracking his back.

“Jariko’s upstairs - go and get him so we can head to the Colosseum.” Irabella forcibly began pushing Kellarom up the stairs.

“No breakfast?!” Kellarom shouted, sounding genuinely worried.

“We can get food there!” Irabella shouted back up the stairs.

Mutana and Irabella began to compose themselves. Mutana found a jug of water and began washing her face and straightening her robe.

“He's not up here!” Kellarom shouted from the second floor.

“What do you mean?” Mutana replied.

“What do you mean, ‘what do I mean?’ He isn't in our room!” Kellarom shouted, making his way back downstairs.

“Maybe he went to get breakfast?” Irabella suggested.

“He did say he wasn't feeling well last night. Maybe he fell asleep outside,” Mutana said. The three mages left the inn and examined the road outside.

“He ain't out here,” Kellarom said.

"We don't have time to find him, he knows where we will be. Let's just go!" Irabella ordered as Mutana stepped onto the muddy road still looking around for him.

They made their way through the Market District. Kellarom stopped to grab some chicken that was cooked on a stick, eating it as they walked to the Colosseum.

"I hope Jariko's okay," Kellarom said with a full mouth.

"He can look after himself - I'm sure he's fine," Mutana replied, stealing one of Kellarom's chicken sticks from his hand.

The atmosphere was just like that of the last two days: crowds of people, merchants shouting as people walked by, street performers and city guards doing their rounds.

Just like the last few times there was a crowd waiting outside the Colosseum, but again they skipped the line to enter. Irabella and Kellarom said good luck to Mutana as she made her way to the separate section. Irabella and Kellarom climbed the stairs and luckily were able to get the same table they'd had the previous day. It felt strange that Jariko wasn't there and Irabella felt bad that they had left him, but she couldn't afford to be late - today was too important for Mutana. But, without Jariko's company, Kellarom's constant talking was really starting to annoy her.

"What do you think the final challenge will be? How long do you think it will take? What is Mutana gonna do if she wins? I'm still kinda hungry."

Irabella didn't like talking to other people. She liked Mutana and she tolerated Jariko, but she couldn't stand Kellarom's constant chatter. Despite this, she did feel that they were becoming friends and Irabella felt bad for Kellarom; she couldn't imagine what it would be like if she lost Mutana. Reluctantly she gave in to her empathy, although she would have preferred silence, they talked until the tournament started.

The Grandmaster stepped out into the arena and greeted the crowd like he had done before.

"Welcome one and all to the final day of our competition. It has been a hard few days. A lot of our participants have tasted defeat, and some have met even worse fates."

Irabella knew Merlon was talking about Moritus and she could see Kellarom welling up in the corner of her eye.

"It has been a great honour for me to have met every single mage who was brave enough to take part, however, only one can prove to themselves and all of us that they are worthy of taking my place, to protect you and all of Concorvia from whatever magical or non-magical threat might appear in the days to come. So, please welcome the final participants." Merlon waved his hand and a band of musicians began playing.

The ominous thudding of the drums and hypnotic whistle from the flutes made the moment feel triumphant and as the music reached its crescendo, the three mages stepped out dressed in the finest robes, each stepping in time with the beat of the drums. The crowd lost all control. When they reached the Grandmaster, the music abruptly stopped in time with them.

Toralium, Paralom and Mutana stood to attention taking in the roar of the crowd, each looking powerful and also terrified at the coming challenge.

“I just want to say thank you to each of you for your service to Concorvia and your devotion to travel all the way here. I know it hasn't been an easy road for any of you but you're here now and whether you win or lose, your lives will never be the same again,” Merlon smiled as the crowd applauded.

“Now shall we begin the final!” He shouted and the applause became rapidly faster and met with shouts and whistles. Merlon waved his hands to motion to the crowd for silence and they did so in eager anticipation.

“So far, we have seen the power of your mind, the deadliness of your skill and your ability to make hard decisions in times of crisis. However, today I only wish to see your control. You will be facing a dangerous beast and must last as long as possible in the arena without killing the creature or letting it harm anyone else. It will be a team effort. If you are injured, then you are out. The winner is the last person standing. Are you ready?” He asked the participants. They nodded back eagerly.

“Bring out the Drag…” he stopped midsentence. The crowd seemed confused as a little bird flew onto Merlon's shoulder. There was a look of shock and sadness on the Grandmaster’s face, and he then turned to Mutana, and looked at her, from where Irabella sat she couldn't hear what the bird said, or what was said between Mutana and the Grandmaster but she saw Mutana smile an evil yet disappointed smile that Irabella had never seen on her before.

Then, all hell broke loose.

The ground around the Grandmaster began to shake and break apart as he rose from the ground by a few feet. The earth beneath him formed into large stone spikes that he launched at Mutana, the other mages beside her released powerful blasts of magic to destroy the spikes. The crowd cheered, thinking this was part of the show.

“What is going on?” Irabella shouted to Kellarom.

“I don't know, but we need to get down there to help and stop this!”

The two young mages leapt out of their seats and headed for the stairway. It wasn't until a stray fireball exploded and almost hit a few people in the crowd that the civilians realised that something was wrong and began to stampede out of the stadium.

Irabella and Kellarom were luckily already at the bottom of the staircase and were able to get out of the way of the panicking city folk.

“Why is the Grandmaster attacking Mutana?” Irabella asked as they ran through the hallway of the Colosseum trying to find an open gate to the arena.

“I have an idea but I hope I'm wrong!” Kellarom replied, gritting his teeth in anger.

"Wrong about what?"

"Me and Jariko were investigating Sireana Silvertongue for the Grandmaster - we thought she may be involved in my brother's death, and we just saw the Grandmaster attack Mutana."

"What's that got to do with anything?!" Irabella asked. She understood but didn't want to believe it.

"Jariko isn't here. I dunno where he is but that was a messenger bird. I'll bet Jariko found something and couldn't get back here to tell us in time."

"What could he have found?" Irabella asked, praying that her assumption was wrong.

"That Mutana knows something about Sireana... or is Sireana!" Kellarom shouted in anger as they found a gate and ran into the ensuing battle.

All the mages that were present in the Colosseum were involved in the battle now.

Half of the mages in the battle had a strange look on their face, almost as if they didn't want to fight, she had heard stories about Sireana Silvertongue and what she was capable of but never thought it would be true. She wondered if it was true, how could Mutana have hidden this kind of power from her.

"Don't use lethal force, they aren't in their right minds," the Grandmaster shouted. "That is Sireana Silvertongue. She's able to bewitch anyone with that necklace she wears. If you engage, don't let her speak."

Irabella had never seen such a battle, mages were battling in the air, while others were hurling lightning at one another, and some were fiercely battling with weapons made of pure energy. The Grandmaster, a master of Class Two magic like Irabella, was flying around and searching for Sireana but he kept getting attacked by the mages protecting her.

Suddenly Irabella found her - she was just about to kill a young mage before Irabella and Kellarom ran to stop her.

"Mutana! What's going on?" Irabella shouted. Tears filled her eyes, a look of betrayal on her face. Mutana turned, burning fire still in her hand facing the young man.

"I'm sorry Irabella, I hoped you would never find out," Sireana said, actually sounding saddened by the events.

"But we've been together for four years! How can Mutana not be a real person?"

"Mutana is the real me. Sireana is my old life. After today - this last job - we can go back to our lives. I just need your help one last time," she extinguished the fire in her hand and began walking over to Irabella with the same hand stretched out towards her.

Irabella didn't know what to do. She began shaking and her eyes continued to stream tears as she looked upon this woman who was like a mother to her. She didn't know what to do until suddenly Kellarom snapped Irabella back into reality.

“You killed my brother, you bitch!” Kellarom exploded from behind her, wielding his staff in his hand, a glowing blue blade on the end of it and bringing it down aiming for Sireana’s head. Sireana jumped back and the two began to battle. Kellarom fought with such ferocity that Sireana was being pushed back. Kellarom was actually trying to kill her and he almost did until Irabella caught his staff and pulled Kellarom back. Sireana smiled.

“I'm glad to see you forgive me,” Sireana said with a soft voice, however, Irabella's face was not that of forgiveness but of rage.

“You’re wrong. I just want to see you in jail, not dead.” As she said this, Irabella lifted Sireana in the air, squeezing her hands together and crushing Sireana and stopping her from breathing. Sireana could not defend herself.

She began to panic and yelled, “Kellarom! Bring this place down!” And with that one command Irabella saw as Kellarom’s eyes glazed over and he stood up.. He raised his staff into the air, screaming and slamming the end down to the ground. As he did so, rocks began to move around the arena, large chunks of earth peeled from the ground and began to form around Kellarom.

The battling around them stopped. All of the mages watched in amazement as a thirty foot stone Golem formed around Kellarom’s body. It was his brother's technique and he had performed it flawlessly, however, Kellarom took it one step further and as the massive stone fist raised in the air a gigantic glowing blue energy sword appeared in the stone figure’s hand and every person inside the Colosseum froze, as they looked upon what could only be described as an avatar of destruction brought its hand down to the ground at high speed.

All Irabella heard was the Grandmaster yell, “Everybody down!” as the giant sword hit the ground. It hit with such devastation that it took half of the Colosseum with it.

Irabella saw the flash of light and was barely able to make a shield for herself in time, however, it wasn't enough, and the blast threw her against the wall, almost knocking her out.

She looked around in a daze and she saw the Grandmaster standing with his arms out and almost all of the mages behind him, protected from the blast, although the strength of his shield had taken a toll on Merlon and his old legs began to shake as he fell to the ground.

Irabella then saw Kellarom standing in the centre of the arena, his giant Golem crumbling away as he picked Sireana up and she heard her say, “Take me to the Grandmaster’s chamber.”

Kellarom put Sireana’s arm around his head and began to guide her to the passage the Grandmaster had shown them the other day. Irabella had no idea what Sireana was planning or how to save Kellarom from her spell. Irabella began to cry, not from the unbearable pain she felt in her back but the pain she felt inside, knowing her best friend and idol had lied to her from the start.

Irabella continued to cry until she heard a strange sound, a sweet chirp from a bird sitting on a rock a few feet from her. Irabella used all her strength to stretch out for the bird and he flew over and sat on her finger, "Did Jariko send you?" She asked with a rough voice, still coughing from the dust in the air. The bird looked at her, tilted its head and chirped.

Irabella took that as a yes. She realised that the bird flew to the Grandmaster so it must be his bird and came from his private chamber.

That must be where Jariko is and they're heading straight for him! she thought, realising the danger he was in. With her last few moments of consciousness, She pulled the bird in closer and said. "Tell him they're coming."

Bird flew off as if all this death and destruction had never happened, just a happy little bird. This was the last thing that Irabella saw as her eyes closed and she whispered, "I'll be there soon, Jariko."

Chapter Twenty-Five: Confrontation

Jariko was in shock. He couldn't move his feet and his breathing was rapid. He knew that the message meant Sireana but who else? He was sweating as the fear wrapped around his neck suffocating him. He slumped back down on the floor trying to calm himself down, then after a few minutes for no apparent reason he found himself thinking about Bombo, the Ogre he met when they fought the Roach-lins. The image of his lovable Ogre friend seemed to calm him down enough for Jariko to remember the scar he had on his hand - the mark he had given himself, so he always remembered his vow to protect others no matter what. He took four deep breaths, and he could feel his heart slowing down. His throat cleared and he found a sudden surge of strength. He jumped to his feet.

Okay, so if Sireana and someone else are on their way here, I can't beat them in a fight alone so I'll have to separate them. The other person is probably just under Sireana's spell so I only have to knock them out and hold Sireana here until some mages get here to stop her, Jariko thought.

Jariko took another few deep breaths before heading downstairs. He didn't know exactly where they would be coming from, but he guessed that they would be coming through the tunnel that leads to the Cosilica and to the Grandmaster's home upstairs, which meant they would pass through the library.

There's no way to know for sure, but if the Grandmaster sent the message he must have known where I was and that they are heading this way. Jariko prayed that he was right and hid behind one of the bookshelves near the centre of the room and waited.

A little time passed before Jariko heard voices coming from behind the door that led to the secret tunnel. His heart began racing in his chest. He quickly pulled out his medicine and took a healthy gulp of it while he had the chance.

Then he heard someone yelling, but he couldn't make out what they were saying until the door exploded open and a six foot tall stone golem came stumbling through.

“Thank you Kellarom, now all we have to do is find the way to Merlon’s room,” a familiar voice said.

Jariko peeked through a gap between some books and saw Sireana standing on the other side of the same bookshelf. Jariko became nervous and tried to slow his breathing, he needed to wait for the perfect moment to try and knock Kellarom out so he didn't have to fight his friend. Sireana and Kellarom walked around the room looking for any way to get upstairs. Jariko avoided their line of sight and kept moving with them until they found the ladder leading upstairs. Sireana must have noticed that the hatch was already open but made her way up the ladder. Just as Kellarom was about to climb up, Jariko pulled out his axe and hit Kellarom with the wooden handle knocking him out, catching him before he hit the ground. Jariko's eyes darted to the hatch but Sireana had already made her way up the creaking stairs that layed beyond the ladder to the hatch. Jariko could hear every step. He quickly laid Kellarom down on the ground and followed Sireana upstairs hoping that she would mistake him for Kellarom. Once Jariko reached the top, he saw Sireana leaning against the table waiting for him.

“Don't think you were going to sneak up on me - the door had been smashed, plus someone sent the bird to Merlon. I knew you were here, Jariko,” Sireana said with a smile. Jariko said nothing as he didn’t think he would get this far. He didn't know what to say.

"Don't worry, I'm not going to bewitch you. It doesn't seem to work, which means you don't find me attractive or you really are just special."

"What do you mean?" Jariko asked.

"I'm guessing you know about my Artifact," she said while playing with the necklace around her neck. "Artifacts are extremely powerful enchanted items. This one makes me the single most beautiful woman to anyone who would find me even slightly attractive. The fun part is that if it does affect someone then they will do literally anything I ask, purely out of love. Which means every man I encounter is my puppet and even some women, but not you." She stood up and walked over to the balcony.

"I've been trying to test it on you since the moment we met, but it never worked, which is strange. You're definitely old enough to find me attractive and you're not gay because I've seen the way you look at Irabella. So, what is your secret?" Jariko slowly began to step into the room, his axe ready.

"I don't know, maybe you're just not as pretty as you think you are." His bravery was a surprise even to himself - to insult a women who could literally melt him was stupid, but something inside him gave him an unusual amount of confidence.

Leaning in the doorway, Sireana's green skin glowed in the sunlight as she laughed and gave Jariko a slow clap.

"Very clever," she said.

Upset by her cockiness, Jariko's patience ran out.

"Why have you done all this? You lied to us! You killed Moritus and Sheladon and now putting innocents in danger! What are you after?"

Sireana sighed and walked over to the bed, sat down and crossed her legs very dramatically.

"We have some time, take a seat." She gestured to the chair by the big table in the centre of the room. Jariko slowly made his way over to it and took a seat, still wielding his axe.

"When I was young I worked for some very bad people - criminals, corrupt lords and bandits. I was poor. I did anything I could for gold. I even killed. I was a good criminal, traveling the world and never getting caught. There aren't many criminal mages, most of them are too loyal to the Creators," she said, rolling her eyes at their ignorance.

"Magic is a gift, and I could make a lot more money as a criminal than I ever could as a priest. That was until I was approached by a creepy guy saying he wanted me to work for their organisation."

"What organisation?" Jariko interrupted.

"They don't have a name, but they are essentially a cult that worships Tando."

"Why worship the trickster god?" He said with surprise.

"A lot of people think it's thanks to him that we were all created in the first place, my darling. Anyway, this cult approached me about stealing various Artifacts from around the world for them. I agreed and I worked for them for years, until I found this one." She held up the necklace as she spoke. "Once I figured out how it worked and how powerful it was, I knew I could change my life with it."

"Let me guess - you never gave it to them?"

"It was never theirs to have - I stole it! It was my right to keep it!" She yelled back. "I used it to make a new life for myself, and I turned into Mutana. Then I met Irabella and she changed me. Just a little snot-nosed kid in the gutter, but I took her in anyway and I loved her." Sireana's eyes dropped to the floor sadly.

"So, why do this. Why kill innocent people?" Jariko yelled at her in frustration.

"Because they found me. They knew about Irabella and they would kill her if I didn't pay back my debt. But they didn't want the necklace. They wanted something in here."

"So, that's why you entered the competition?"

"That was their idea too - friends in high places, I guess."

Jariko was beginning to understand her. She just wanted to be happy and have a normal life but the world's cruelty sculpted her.

"What about the Roach-lins? That day in the tunnel, they were looking for you?"

"Honestly, I'm not too sure. I know this cult has some kind of understanding with the Roach-lins, so it was probably part of a greater plan. Or, perhaps they intended to double cross me. Who knows?" Sireana said, shrugging.

"Okay, so what now?" Jariko asked.

"I find what they want and leave forever." She paused for a moment after saying this as a tear ran down her face.

"Just promise me you will look after Irabella. I never wanted it to go this far. I just wanted to protect her."

Jariko nodded slowly then asked, "What do they want?"

Sireana smiled, "That's not for you to know Jariko. Come to think of it, it's probably time I looked for it. I think it's time you left."

Sireanas' face turned serious as she hurtled an apple-sized fireball at Jariko's chest. It exploded, and the shock wave scattered everything on the table and threw Jariko against the wall.

"I'm sorry Jariko, but I need to look after myself now. There's no hiding from these people." Sireana threw another fireball, but Jariko was able to bat it away with his axe.

"Just stop and explain yourself to the Grandmaster. He will help you!" He shouted.

"What and go to jail? I'm dead either way, at least this way I have a fighting chance," She launched two more fireballs from each hand. Jariko dived out of the way and rolled to his feet as the two fireballs hit the back wall leaving black scorch marks.

“You don’t have to die here Jariko. Just leave.”

“I can't let you get away!”

Jariko leapt into the air with his axe above his head. Sireana exploded a fireball that was in her hand, the shock wave throwing Jariko back into the wall again.

“You don't understand the power these people have! If I go to jail the same thing that happened at Rybalin will happen here, just to get to me!”

“Then help the Grandmaster take whoever is in charge down!” Jariko struggled to his feet using his axe to help him up, but Sireana walked over, kicking him and putting her foot on his chest.

“No one knows who's in charge. Whoever it is, they are beyond powerful. This cult is worldwide and dates back a long time. Trust me Jariko, you can't take them down,” Sireana raised her flaming hand once again inches from Jariko’s face.

“I'm sorry…” Jariko closed his eyes but nothing happened.

Sireana's foot disappeared as she was thrown across the room, slamming into the wall above the fireplace. Jariko looked to the balcony and saw Merlon standing in the doorway leaning on Irabella’s shoulder. They both looked half dead, but Jariko figured out why the staircase was so unused - the Grandmaster must be able to fly to the balcony. This time, it looked like he needed Irabella's help to make it.

"Jariko!" Irabella shouted and ran over to him.

"Don't worry about me - Kellarom's downstairs," he replied.

Irabella nodded as she left. Her and Sireana's eyes met and Jariko had never seen that much fire and anger in a woman's eyes before. Even he was scared of what Irabella would do, but she continued to run down the staircase to the ladder back to the library, worried for her friend. Jariko looked back over to Sireana. Her eyes were fixed on the doorway and tears were running down her face. She had done too much to be forgiven.

Sireana composed herself and stood up, "Hello, Merlon. You don't look very good."

"How could you have done this?!" Merlon yelled, coughing into his hand as he fell to one knee.

"None of you are looking too good, but even so, two against one isn't fair," Sireana said as Jariko and Merlon both climbed to their feet to face her.

"Two men against one woman, I'm flattered but I'm not really in the mood," she smiled and laughed to herself before raising her finger and wagged it at them.

"No, no, no, I have a better idea," Sireana smiled.

"You know Jariko, my charm might not work on you, but it does work on him. Merlon... kill Jariko."

Chapter Twenty-Six: No Holding Back

Jariko didn't even have time to react before the table in front of him was thrown in his direction, slamming into him and throwing him to the ground.

Jariko recoiled in pain as several other objects from around the room hurtled towards him, hit after hit. Jariko had no idea how he was going to stop the Grandmaster - he was the most powerful mage in Concorvia. Jariko could see Sireana searching the room. She looked everywhere but defeat was painted on her face. Jariko wondered what exactly it was that she needed.

"Merlon, where is it?" Sireana shouted.

"Where's what, my darling?" He responded while halting his assault.

"Agorith's Legacy?"

"I have no idea what that is," Merlon replied in confusion. On the other side of the room, while they were talking Jariko had been able to get to his feet. Merlon turned back around, and anger swelled on his face as he began waving his hand violently back and forth throwing everything he could see at Jariko, but this time Jariko was ready. He gripped his axe until his knuckles turned white and swung faster and faster, batting away everything the Grandmaster threw at him.

Jariko began to inch his way forward, slowly but surely, and Sireana began to panic.

"Just throw him out of the window!" She screamed.

Jariko panicked as he watched the Grandmaster point his hand towards Jariko and flick his wrist towards the window. Jariko closed his eyes waiting for the magical force to sweep him off his feet and launch him out of the window, but it never happened. Merlon tried again but Jariko did not move. Jariko was confused for a moment, but a smile grew on his face when he realised that Merlon must be fighting Sireana's control.

Jariko took the opportunity and swung the blunt end of his axe to knock Merlon out, but his axe stopped in mid-air. Merlon couldn't throw Jariko but his axe was a different matter.

He raised his hand high above his head and Jariko's axe raised higher and higher. Jariko refused to let go, and after a few moments Jariko was dangling close to the ceiling, clinging to his axe for dear life. Merlon began swinging his hand back and forth and the axe copied, trying to loosen Jariko's grip until eventually Jariko's finger betrayed him and he let go.

Jariko was flung through the air like a ragdoll slamming into the wall above the fireplace and hitting the concrete ground hard. The wind was knocked out of his chest and he gasped for air while waiting for the inevitable chop of his axe to bring his life to an end.

It never came: his axe fell to the ground with an ear-piercing clang and Jariko looked up to see Sireana and

Merlon staring at the wall above him. Jariko could barely see straight but as he focused his eyes on his opponents, it looked like they had seen a ghost.

Jariko stumbled to his feet and turned around. The wall above the fireplace where he'd been slammed into had crumbled away revealing a cavity behind the brickwork. It looked like this section was specifically designed to hide a secret.

As Jariko's eyes focused on the cavity in the wall, he could see glowing writing written on the brickwork of a secret cavity in the wall that looked as if it had been written moments ago, but from the look on the Grandmaster's face, he had no idea this message existed. Sireana's face was a different matter; this is what she had been looking for. It read:

"You are of the right mind, but in the wrong place,

What you wish to find, is in another time and space.

A shipwreck unfound, a crew lost to sea,

Find the cursed one bound, you are but a flea.

He won't let you take it, be ready for a fight,

You must make him submit, or be ready to take flight.

You will receive a gift, a reminder of the Pantheon,

Take care not to go adrift on your quest for the Astrotheon."

Jariko's eyes showed nothing but confusion as he turned to look at Sireana and Merlon. Sireana was smiling uncontrollably, whilst Merlon on the other hand had pure dread across his face which sent a chill down Jariko's spine. What could be so bad to scare Merlon?

Sireana turned to Jariko, "Thank you!" she said with an incredulous laugh, "For finding this I'll give you a chance to live. However, since I'm not going to be the next Grandmaster, I better destroy the evidence. You should leave the tower."

Sireana turned to Merlon.

"Get me out of here, but first, bring the tower down."

Within moments, Sireana and Merlon lifted from the balcony. Jariko ran out and watched as they levitated a short distance into the sky before stopping and turning to face him while suspended. Irabella and Kellarom came running up the stairs.

"Jariko! What happened?" Irabella shouted. Kellarom still looked dazed and then confused when he saw the message.

"Quick! Memorise it before they destroy it!" Jariko shouted, moments later a large crack began forming around the room.

"We have to go!" Jariko shouted. "Merlon is gonna bring down the tower!"

Irabella's face didn't register what he said until it was too late. The roof of the room lifted up high into the sky revealing Merlon and Sireana flying above them. Loose rocks fell from the now flying roof and landed on the three friends. Kellarom only just managed to jump into the stairway before a large piece of concrete fell from the sky, blocking the door and badly injuring Irabella's leg. Irabella screamed in pain as the shard of rock tore into her leg and collapsing to the floor.

"Creators, damn it!" Jariko shouted. "Can you walk?"

He started to panic, grabbing a blanket and trying to bandage her leg as best he could.

"We can't get out of here, Jariko," Irabella said, recoiling from the pain.

Kellarom shouted from the other side of the concrete slab, "Jariko, I can't move it!"

Grunts of strength and pain came from the other side but the concrete slab wouldn't move and Kellaroms type of magic was too destructive to move it without hurting his friends. Jariko knew he could move it, but not in time to get Irabella out as well.

"Just run Kell - get outta here!"

Kellarom began screaming as he desperately tried to move the concrete slab.

Sireana looked down at the helpless children and a tear fell from her face once again. She had to destroy the evidence and her chance to escape would quickly disappear, she had to do it, she silently said.

“I'm sorry” to Irabella before turning to Merlon.

“Do it.” Merlon slapped his hand together and the ceiling crushed and twisted into a large concrete ball, and as if he was dropping a marble, he released his fingers and the concrete boulder fell from the sky.

Jariko's eyes widened as he saw it fall, his mind emptied, and he readied himself.

Irabella couldn't bring herself to say anything, she couldn't even scream in fear as the boulder fell towards them. She simply closed her eyes, the last thing she would see was Jariko standing over her like the hero he was and realising she would never get to tell him how she felt.

A few moments passed and she felt it hit. It crashed with an almighty thud and she could hear the Cosilica buckle under the weight, but she felt no pain. She was still alive.

Irabella slowly opened her eyes and just like before she saw Jariko standing over her, but this time it was different. Jariko’s poncho was flung over his shoulder like a cape and four pulsating arms protruded from Jariko's torso, his face red from the strain, his legs cracking the floor he was standing on as he had caught the enormous boulder.

“You're a Giant!” Irabella screamed in shock and fear, however, Jariko didn’t respond. He tilted his body to the left and with all of his remaining strength took four agonising steps to the edge of the building before leaning to one side and throwing the boulder just far enough to land safely in the open fields below.

"What's going on?!" She screamed, completely disregarding what had just happened. Jariko turned to her and smiled, holding up his two right arms with a thumbs up on each, before falling back on the ground.

Irabella looked up, but Merlon and Sireana had already gone. They disappeared as soon as the giant boulder dropped to cover their escape. She looked over to the wall, but the message had been destroyed. She wanted to write it down, but she could feel her eyes growing heavy. She was exhausted and badly hurt. Irabella crawled her way over to Jariko, every movement sending an agonising jolt through her, and began crying.

"Thank you," she whispered, kissing him on the cheek before passing out herself.

Chapter Twenty-Seven: King's Call

Jariko awakened in a panic, jumping from the bed and onto the ground. Kellarom tried to catch him.

"Woah! Everything is okay Jariko - we won, well, we kinda won."

Jariko looked around confused. The last thing he remembered was the boulder falling towards him. A few moments later Jariko realised he wasn't wearing his poncho and his arms were on show in all their glory. Jariko recoiled and leapt to the other side of the bed trying to hide from Kellarom's sight.

"You've been unconscious for two days Jariko. Don't worry, I've had plenty of time to come to grips with... this." Kellarom gestured towards Jariko. "To be honest, it makes a lot of sense. I knew a Human couldn't be that strong."

"You're not scared of me? Or gunna try and kill me?" Jariko asked slowly standing up.

"Why would I be scared of you? I'm a pointy-eared, green-skinned Goblin. Cross breeding is nothing new Jariko. Orcs are a mix of Goblins and Elves, although we came from the same Creator. Crossing traits from Humans and Giants has never been seen before. Both species come from different Creators so the base make up shouldn't match enough to create life."

Jariko sat back down on the bed. He was in immense pain from multiple broken ribs and his head was beating like a drum. He started rubbing his head before interrupting Kellarom's chain of thought.

"Where's Irabella? Is she okay?" Jariko asked standing up again, although this time too quickly and he became dizzy. Kellarom grabbed one of his arms to steady him and laid him back down.

"She's fine. She woke up a few hours after the incident. We were all just a bit tired, but you completely exhausted yourself."

"My medicine?"

"It's right here," Kellarom grabbed the small bottle from the table and Jariko took a drink.

"Makes sense now - sugar water, lots of food and oversleeping," Kellarom said grinning.

"What?" Jariko asked.

"It makes sense. Because you're half Giant you're insanely strong, but because you're half human so your body is small. So, your medicine is just to stop your body from running out of energy. It's the same reason you can eat like a starved tiger and sleep like a bear," Kellarom laughed. "I should have been able to figure it out days ago, although I think Merlon figured it out quite quickly."

Jariko suddenly remembered what had happened.

"Is the Grandmaster okay? What did Sireana do with him?"

"He's fine too. Once he flew her out the city, she just told him to return. I'm guessing killing the Grandmaster would have made her too much of a target," Kellarom said spitting on the ground, his face turning red with anger. The room was still for a few moments before Jariko broke the silence.

"I'm sorry we couldn't stop her," Jariko said looking down at the floor in shame.

"Don't be sorry, you figured out who she was. If it wasn't for you, she would be Grandmaster right now and Concorvia would be in very big trouble."

“But I wanted to help you avenge your brother’s death,” Jariko said, tearing up. Kellarom put his arm around Jariko’s shoulder and started tearing up himself. He rubbed his eyes with his sleeve.

“Don't worry about that. I'm gonna hunt that bitch until the day I die.”

Kellarom and Jariko looked at each other and began laughing.

“I’m in!” Jariko said as the two boys slapped their hands together and hugged. Irabella walked into the room and the two boys both panicked, pushing off one another and wiping the tears from their faces.

“Were you having a moment?” Irabela asked mockingly.

The boys simultaneously answered, “NO!”

Irabella laughed before walking over to Jariko and hugging him. It didn't seem like she was affected by the sight of him whatsoever and this comforted Jariko. He hadn't felt this comfortable since he was home with his mother. No one had ever known he was a Giant except old man Rolo. He had helped Jariko’s mother through his birth. No one else had ever known Jariko's secret. His mother made him swear he would never take off his poncho around people and to never tell anyone, although Jariko was struggling to understand why. Kellarom and Irabella didn't seem to care at all.

“So, you guys are okay with what I am?” Jariko asked standing up and limping over to his poncho then throwing it on.

"It was a shock, but I quickly got over it. It made a lot of sense once I thought about it," Irabella replied and Kellarom shouted out.

"That's what I said!"

The three continued to discuss the events of the past few days. Jariko explained how he figured it out and Irabella told him what had happened at the Colosseum. Jariko was impressed with Kellarom's power.

"Yeah, I didn't know I could do that either. I tried to recreate it, but it didn't work. Merlon said the Artifact she used brought out some kind of hidden power of love, like a mother protecting her baby. That's how I was able to push past my limits."

That's a very dangerous Artifact, Jariko thought as the door to his chamber opened, it was Merlon.

"Ah, you're awake. Good to see you my boy," Merlon shouted, smiling and running over to hug him.

"Who knew you had such a gift... in investigation," Merlon said winking as a guard walked in behind him.

"There is a messenger from Commander Claypius. I'll spare you the details - he wants you three to meet him at the king's palace in the Royal District tonight."

Jariko, Kellarom and Irabella were all speechless for a moment.

"Why?" Irabella asked.

"Well, first you guys saved lives at Rybalin, then you saved the whole capital from a dangerous criminal. The king was very impressed to hear your tales of victory and wants to thank you himself."

The room was silent before the messenger spoke up in a very well-spoken voice.

"How would you like to respond?" He asked, bowing down low.

"Of course!" Jariko shouted before Irabella elbowed him in the ribs.

Then she returned the bow and then spoke just as politely, "We would be honoured to meet the king tonight."

Jariko and Kellarom looked at each other and copied her bow. The messenger gave an obnoxious smile and left the room.

"So, how are you feeling?" Merlon asked.

"Better. I'm sorry about your home, Grandmaster," Jariko said, feeling ashamed and defeated.

"Don't worry about it Jariko. I was the one to destroy it, remember," Merlon said, laughing before his face turned serious.

"I acted rashly. I underestimated the power of the Artifact and almost killed all of you. If it wasn't for your remarkable heritage, I would be standing at your graves. I should be thanking you." Merlon looked genuinely sad at just the thought of this, and Jariko could tell he was punishing himself for being used like a puppet so easily.

"Sir?" Kellarom whispered to the Grandmaster.

"Yes, Kellarom?" Merlon replied.

"What about the riddle? It's what she was after the whole time - what's the Astrotheon?"

Merlon leant in and gestured for them all to copy him. Then he began to whisper, "Let's not speak of it here. Meet me tomorrow morning and we will discuss the ramifications of what has happened. I'm sorry to say your Fates are now intertwined with the events to come." This scared Jariko just as much as it confused him. The Grandmaster continued, "For now, just prepare to meet the king. Here's some coins. Relax for today - it's going to be your last chance for a while."

This perplexed them even more, but before they could ask, Merlon left smiling like nothing had happened.

"So, what now?"Jariko asked.

"Well, let's go into the city and get ready to meet the king and Commander Claypius, and I guess relax," Irabella said, picking up her bag.

"To be fair, I'm starving!" Kellarom yelled, rubbing his stomach and they all laughed.

They spent the next few hours roaming the city. Irabella bought new clothes. She felt that she wasn't an apprentice anymore; she didn't really feel part of the Church after the betrayal of Sireana, so she decided for now she would wear some common clothes with leather boots and a jacket. The boys liked the new look. They held up their thumbs in approval, and Irabella returned with her middle finger.

Kellarom decided to spend his money on as much food as he could fit in his bag or his mouth. He was so worried about Jariko not waking up he had barely eaten for days.

Jariko decided he didn't want to buy anything, instead he went out to the main gates and spent some time with Runner, his lovable horse he had left with the generous stableman who wasn't too happy to see Jariko after days of looking after his horse, however, once Jariko handed him the bag of coins he quickly forgot about the hell Runner had put him through the past few days.

As the sun began to set, the group headed through the city, all the way to the centre of the capital. They were all so nervous they barely spoke on the walk. None of them had met a king before. They made their way past the Colosseum until they found themself at the crossing in the road. One direction led down to the east side of the Grand District and eventually back to the Market District, but the other road led past the Cosilica and to the gate of the Royal District. They followed the road up the hill until they were standing outside the smallest district in the city and directly in front of them was the King's Palace.

Chapter Twenty-Eight: Keepers of Concorvia

Jariko had never laid eyes on the palace before. From where he was standing it looked like something from a fairy tale. The palace looked like it was carved from marble, every window expertly carved and detailed with golden frames. The actual shape of the castle was wide at the base, the centre building stretching high into the sky turning into a pointed roof at the top and wing-like sections stretching out to the sides that followed the cone-shaped centre, each floor getting smaller and smaller.

As they approached the gate, two heavily armoured guards stopped them, holding Halberd spears in their way.

"Halt, where do you think you are going?" One of the guards asked.

"Commander Claypius asked us to meet him here tonight," Irabella replied politely.

"Oh, you are the three heroes? You're so young." He coughed awkwardly and pulled his spear back to his side.

"Go on through. The Commander is waiting for you in the entrance."

They passed through the gate and Kellarom felt the need to lightly tap the guard's helmet.

"Cheers," Kellarom said, smiling as he arrogantly walked through. He couldn't see the guard's face but his eyes didn't look happy.

The entrance to the palace was at the top of a large half circle shaped stone staircase that they climbed while taking in their surroundings. Either side of them was a magnificent garden with flowers of every colour, arranged to look otherworldly. Jariko definitely didn't feel like he was still on his own planet. How could Primak look so beautiful? He was so used to seeing the mud-covered streets of Rybalin and the Market District, he never imagined a place could look so beautiful and peaceful.

They approached the large black obsidian doors and two guards heaved the doors open for them and there was Commander Claypius, waiting for them on the other side.

"Ah, welcome Jariko, and welcome to your friends as well. I don't think we have been formally introduced. I'm Commander Claypius. Don't worry about telling me your names, I am well aware who you all are," Claypius said smiling, he was still wearing his plated armour.

"Please follow me, the king would like to explain everything himself."

Claypius waved his hand and began to lead them through the hall. Just like the outside the hall looked as if it was made entirely of marble. Large columns holding the ceiling up and red carpets running through every doorway like roads in a field. They followed the Commander to the other end of the hall until they reached large golden doors with a lion carved into its surface.

“Don't be scared, just stand there and listen,” Claypius said reassuringly and pushed the doors open. Behind the doors was revealed to be the throne room. It was just like the main hall but in the centre of the room the marble floor curved up to a stepped platform where a golden throne sat and upon the golden throne was the king.

Jariko wasn't really interested in politics. He had never bothered to learn about his king or any of the kings before him, but at this moment he greatly regretted this. He had no idea how to act or what to say if asked a question. What scared him the most was that the man on the throne didn't look like a king. Claypius and all the other guards were in ceremonial armour and decorated head to toe, but the man in front of Jariko couldn't have been further from them. He had long scruffy swept back ginger hair down to his shoulders, he was clean shaven but scars riddled his face. He wore common clothes, thick leather boots and a long leather coat with a fur collar that draped down the side of the throne. The only thing that made him look like a king was the golden amulet around his neck with a lion's face carved into it. Jariko recognized the lion design from Commander Claypius’ chest plate.

“You three must be who I have heard so much about,” the king shouted with a deep and piercing voice. “From what I've heard, you have outdone my guards twice over."

His gaze fixed on Jariko, making him squirm uncomfortably.

"That is no surprise to me," the king said as he raised himself from the throne, laughing as he did so. "I am not surprised with this guy in charge."

He patted Claypius on the back still laughing. Jariko, Irabella and Kellarom were so shocked they didn't know how to react. Was this actually the king? He walked up to them and stood just an arm's length away.

"I'm sorry - I am King Leo," he bowed and the three returned the bow, Jariko got the sense he wasn't a normal king. "I know I may not seem like a king, but Claypius and I grew up on the battlefield. I wasn't raised in these halls, those fancy kings from the fairytales don't actually exist. They're just the fantasy of the people who wrote about them," he said, chuckling to himself.

Jariko was speechless, but he felt more at ease now.

"Now to the matter at hand," King Leo took a seat on one of the steps behind him. "Rybalin was destroyed and you were the first on the scene, saving dozens of people and destroying a Roach-lin nest. Then you took it upon yourself to help the Grandmaster to find a dangerous criminal even though he never actually wanted your help. You found the criminal and though you weren't able to catch her, you were able to thwart her plans to gain a seat of power in my city and uncovered a scheme to find a great power by a dangerous cult we weren't even aware existed. Have I missed anything?"

The three stood silent.

Then, Irabella decided to speak.

"Actually your highness, Jariko did almost all of it, we were just involved."

King Leo smiled, "No need to be so formal, Leo is fine."

Irabella blushed.

"As for what you said, I already know. Every witness we have spoken to including the Grandmaster has explained each scenario in great detail and Jariko, you were always the talking point. Nevertheless, anyone who is willing to fight for the lives of others, whether they play a large or small part, still deserves recognition. Besides, I'm sure Jariko couldn't have done what he did without your help. Would you agree, Jariko?" Jariko nodded nervously.

"Yes, your high… Leo… I never would have been in Rybalin if it wasn't for Irabella, plus I never would have caught Sireana if Kellarom had not noticed his brother's death wasn't an accident,"

Leo smiled and stood up.

"No man is an army. Oh, and that reminds me," he walked over to Kellarom, placing a hand on his shoulder. "I have arranged for your brother to be buried here in the city. I know what losing a brother is like."

Kellarom refused to cry but managed to say, “Thank you,” as a single tear snuck out and ran down his cheek.

As Leo sat back down, Claypius spoke up from the corner of the room.

“Leo..” He said as he gestured that he was needed to be somewhere else.

“Oh, yes, sorry I get side-tracked sometimes. I called you here because I need gifted people to follow up on the events that have transpired. Merlon has explained to me the message you found and what that could mean for Concorvia so I'm here to ask you for your help. We haven't got the manpower to spare right now - the refugees from Rybalin are defenceless and our mage forces are pushing back the Roach-lin infestation, however, this cult that Sireana has found herself conspiring with needs to be dealt with and I need you three to do what you can to stop it. I know you're young, but I have arranged with the Grandmaster to prepare you the best he can. I only ask you to do what you can to get more information and potentially stop whatever it is they are planning. Will you help?”

Jariko, Irabella and Kellarom looked at each other and without saying a word all three silently agreed and nodded.

“Brilliant,” Leo shouted, smiling and clapping his hands together. “In that case, there is one last thing.”

King Leo stood up and pushed his long leather coat back revealing a sword that Jariko hadn't even noticed he was wearing until that moment. He unsheathed his blade and said.

“Please kneel,” the three did as he asked and got down onto one knee.

“I, King Leo the Sixth, rightful king of Concorvia and member of the Council of Five Titans, knight you Keepers of Concorvia, my knights that shine light in the darkest places. Protect those who need protecting and kill those who wish us harm. May the Creators guide you and Primak protect you.”

As he was saying this, he placed his blade on Jariko's right shoulder, then moved it to his left and back to his right. He repeated this process for Irabella and Kellarom before sheathing his blade.

“Now, arise,” Leo shouted dramatically and chuckled to himself. He walked over to a guard who was holding a small wooden box. He took the box from him and walked back over and opened it.

“These medallions are badges of office. Anywhere you need to go in Concorvia, these should allow you access. Just remember to say, ‘I am on the king’s business for the security of Concorvia.’ I'm sure they will come in handy.” Leo put each medallion around each of their necks, with a look of pride on his face. It was the same lion design that Leo wore himself, however, the golden coin was much smaller, no larger than a normal gold coin.

“Now I am sorry, I do have to go, but Merlon will tell you everything you need to know, we have already discussed the implications of the last few days and your part you have yet to play," he said as he handed the box back to the guard and walked past them, but then stopped. "I am truly in your debt. Concorvia thanks all three of you," Leo gave the group a final affectionate look before being escorted out by Claypius.

Jariko wasn't surprised that he was busy, but he was disappointed he couldn't speak to King Leo for longer.

"I can't believe he knighted us!" Kellarom shouted in excitement. Jariko returned the excitement, remembering old stories of the keepers who travelled the land protecting the people of Concorvia however they could.

"I never thought I would ever be knighted," Jariko said while admiring the medallion around his neck. Irabella was silent but Jariko could see the excitement on her face.

"Come on!" Kellarom said, "Let's go back to the George and have some food. We'll speak to the Grandmaster at first light."

Kellarom led the way. The three Keepers headed back to the inn for a well-deserved celebration.

Chapter Twenty-Nine: The Quest Begins

The next day the sunlight crept through the window and beams of sunlight filled the empty room as Jariko woke up. He laid there thinking about the last few weeks of his life while playing with his new solid gold medallion that hung around his neck. He had never had friends, he had never left the house for longer than a few hours and he had never battled anything larger than a rat. Now he was an adventurer, with two people he would die for, he hadn't been home for weeks and he had battled a Roach-lin king, a powerful sorceress and even the Grandmaster himself. He had met the King of Concorvia and been knighted as its protector and discovered an ancient secret that not even the mages of the church knew about. He knew his mother would be proud and his life was never going to be the same again.

When Jariko decided to head downstairs he saw Irabella already sitting at a table. He waved and made his way through the inn to sit down with her.

"Good morning," Jariko said smiling. Irabella returned the smile but hers came across a little more awkward and forced.

"Morning, I've already ordered breakfast. Is Kellarom on his way?" She asked.

"He was just washing when I left - he will be down soon," Jariko replied while adjusting his chair. They sat there awkwardly for a moment before Jariko decided to speak.

“I'm sorry,” he said.

“What for?” Irabella asked.

“For not telling you that we were looking for Sireana… and then all the stuff that came after.” Jariko's eyes fell to the floor.

“Yeah, I was kinda pissed you guys left me out, but if we are being honest, I wouldn't have helped anyway.”

“Still…” Jariko didn't know what to say, he couldn't imagine what Irabella was going through.

“I owe you one anyway, so call us even,” she replied.

“What for?”

“You caught a two-tone boulder to save me! You could have run.”

Jariko blushed slightly.

“How do you feel about that by the way?” Jariko asked, wiggling his hidden arms under his poncho.

“I've seen weirder.”

“Really?!” Jariko asked.

“I was almost eaten by a cockroach the size of a bear! You're not even in my top five!” They laughed together and then the awkward silence fell again.

Jariko blushed and said, “By the way, thank you for that kiss.”

He started grinning uncontrollably.

“I thought you’d passed out!” She shouted, punching him in the arm.

“I was about to, but it just took a while,” he said recoiling in fear as Irabella was pulling back to deliver another blow. Before she could, Kellarom came downstairs and interrupted.

“Woah, what's going on?”

“Nothing!” Irabella said scowling at Jariko, trying to pretend she wasn't blushing.

Jariko just giggled softly and the three of them continued to talk as their breakfast arrived.

Once they finished their meal, they packed their stuff up and paid the innkeeper for the last few nights.

“Thank you very much! Come back soon!” The innkeeper said.

They waved as they exited the inn and made their way to the Cosilica to meet the Grandmaster. They were shocked to see the top of the tower had already been rebuilt and was good as new. They admired the cathedral for a moment before Jariko noticed the boulder peeking out from behind the back of the Cosilica and silently patted his own back. He had no idea he could lift something of that size.

They arrived and were met by the Grandmaster.

“Ah, welcome. You're all looking well rested.”

He was planting flowers outside the main door as they approached. He put down his gardening tools and waved for them to follow him inside. They made their way through a different section of the Cosilica and into a strange storage room filled from top to bottom with bits and pieces.

“I'm sure King Leo told you everything he was planning. Congratulations Keepers,” he said, chuckling.

“Don't let the title scare you. Most of the work of a Keeper is just to keep the peace and help where you can. Danger of this level is very rare, even in wartime, with Sireana and this strange organisation it is very troubling”

“Is it?” Jariko asked. Merlon looked at him in confusion. “Wartimes?” Jariko added. Merlon sighed deeply.

“I don't know, my boy. Hopefully you can figure that out before it's too late.”

They sat down at a round table and Merlon's face became serious.

“The riddle you found is no laughing matter. It was left there by Agorith himself centuries ago.”

“What for?” Irabella asked.

“The Astrotheon. You see, hundreds of years ago when the Artifacts were being created and Agorith was still the Grandmaster, a great power was discovered called the Astrotheon. We don't know what it is; all mention of it has been erased from history. All we do know is that it turns someone into a god. A war was waged over it and when the war was over, Agorith and the Astrotheon were gone, never to be seen again along with the old city of Orkesta where the Agorith lake lays now. No one even knew if it was real... until now." Jariko was amazed he had never heard of such a thing.

"Is it an Artifact?" asked Jariko.

"No, we don't think it is. Artifacts can only be as powerful as the enchanter, and there has never been a mage powerful enough to create something like that." Merlon's face changed to one of shame and frustration. "We don't know how this cult knew about the message, but the problem is they found it and Sireana is most likely on her way to tell them its location right now, or she's heading to get it herself."

"And what can we do?" Kellarom asked.

"Frankly, my boy, you three are the most gifted children I know. You and Irabella are prodigies at your age and, well we have all seen what Jariko is capable of. You three are our best chance to stop this cult from finding the Astrotheon. I would go myself but as you can imagine I don't get a lot of time for adventuring, and you three will draw a lot less attention than my colleague, plus it will be good experience for you all."

"But where do we start?" Jariko asked. Merlon got out a little notebook that he had written out the riddle onto.

"Well, 'a shipwreck unfound' seems to be the location," Merlon suggested.

“There must be thousands of shipwrecks around the world!” Kellarom yelled, grabbing his head in frustration.

“What about ‘you’re but a flea’?” Irabella asked.

“Well, I would assume it means a size comparison and the only place that has creatures large enough that we would be a flea is the island of Kai-jan.” Merlon replied triumphantly.

“I thought that was a myth?” Jariko asked.

“It's quite real my boy, and it's off the coast of Tortu,” Merlon added, smiling.

“The pirate country to the east? With the crocodile and shark people?”

“They’re alligators! And you shouldn't say stuff like that - they're called the Alutat and Shatorem,” Irabella corrected.

“They would kill us on sight either way!” Kellarom shouted.

“Actually, we are at peace with Tortu at the moment, and the pirate king has been in the Council of Five Titans for the last few years,” Merlon said, stroking his beard.

The room fell silent as they all thought about what this would entail. Not only the danger of traveling to another country, but also fighting a mythical beast and the constant danger of the mysterious cult reappearing. Jariko thought long and hard until he had made up his mind.

"I'll go," he said. As he said this Merlons face lit up with pride.

"I'm in too!" Irabella added.

Kellarom was shocked. He looked at both of them as if they were crazy, but eventually put his hand in the air.

"Fine, I'm in. But only so I get another chance at Sireana!"

Irabella flinched slightly at the name before saying, "Agreed."

"Magnificent!" Merlon shouted as he stood up in excitement. "You three never cease to amaze me," he said smiling from ear to ear. "Don't worry, I won't send you off empty handed," he yelled as he ran off and carried back a large wooden crate. He placed it down on the table in front of them and a plume of dust erupted from inside. He then leant over and handed Irabella the notebook he had written the riddle on.

"This is for you my dear - it's an enchanted notebook. It's only Category one artifact, but it will never run out of space for all your spells and secrets."

Irabella's was breathless as she began to write fiercely in the notebook. Jariko tried to see what she was writing but she covered it with her arm. Merlon then reached into the crate and pulled out a staff with intricate carvings along the shaft and a blue crystal crafted into the tip.

He turned to Kellarom and said, "This is a staff made of toralium, an indestructible metal, and the crystal on the top is made from solid magic, mined from deep beneath the earth. They are called Induliam Crystals. They are extremely powerful and extremely dangerous, but I saw what you did at the tournament. You have the potential to surpass even me and with this staff in your hand that is inevitable. Just focus on the crystal and your spells will be twice as potent."

Kellarom's eyes widened, and he looked like a child on their birthday as he grabbed the staff.

"Take this spell book as well. I noticed neither of you have learnt any Class one magic, so these are some basic spells to learn," Merlon passed the tome to Irabella for safe keeping.

"Thanks, old man!" Kellarom and Irabella both shouted before hugging Merlon. They all laughed before Kellarom began to swing his new staff around the room.

"And finally, Jariko." Merlon reached into the crate and pulled out Jariko's axe. "I think you lost this during the fight."

Jariko smiled.

"Thanks Merlon. I didn't feel right without it."

"I should probably tell you that it is an Artifact," Merlon said.

Jariko's eyes shot at Merlon in surprise.

"What?"

"It can chop any wood in one slice. That's how you were able to break down the enchanted door to my room," Merlon said laughing, Jariko was speechless.

"This whole time we had a powerful artifact?" Jariko said in disbelief as he examined his axe.

"Well, to be honest it only chops wood Jariko. It's not the most powerful enchantment but can be very useful. Plus, it's still rare to find out in the world," Merlon replied smiling. "But you will also need a more powerful item so I do have another gift for you."

He reached in and pulled out a little leather satchel bag, no bigger than a dinner plate.

"This is the most powerful Artifact I have and it's the only Category five artifact I've ever seen. I call it the pit bag."

"You mean it's bottomless?" Jariko exclaimed in excitement, reaching his hand in but he couldn't feel the bottom.

"It's empty right now, but unless someone knows what's inside it, they won't be able to pull anything out. Plus, the inside isn't affected by time so put all of your food in there and it will stay fresh. Just don't forget what you put in there otherwise it will be lost forever. Still, very useful when searching for other artifacts and traveling the world. Your axe may only be Category four but still a worthy piece for a collection."

Jariko admired his new bag before placing his axe inside it and watched as it just disappeared. Jariko knew he would never get used to seeing that. They all thanked Merlon for their gifts and proceeded to the main door.

Just as they reached the big wooden doors leaving the main hall, Jariko noticed the statue staring at him from the other side. He decided to embrace the statue again. He stood before it, closed his eyes and waited, however, this time he felt nothing but happiness and excitement for the adventure to come. He opened his eyes and smiled - he had conquered his demons and he was filled with pride.

As he lit one of the candles he whispered, “I love you Mum, I hope you are watching,” and then ran to catch up with his friends.

They had made their way to the side of the cathedral where Merlon had buried Moritus. Kellarom was on his knees in front of the tombstone with his eyes closed as he was praying with Merlon. Even Irabella couldn't help but cry as Merlon said the prayer.

“A good son, brother and friend, Moritus was taken too soon. You may see his death as a waste, and you may miss him dearly, but it is in our lord Primak that he still lives. He is returned to the earth from which he came and here he shall spend his remaining days, until the earth chooses to reclaim him, and to be reborn once again.”

Jariko felt himself choking up at the memory of his lost friend. The last few days had been enough of a distraction to subdue the feeling of loss.

He felt Irabella's soft hand grab him as she turned and began to cry into his shoulder. They stayed there for over an hour as Kellarom shared stories of his brother, some making the group laugh and others bringing back the tears, but eventually they were ready and Kellarom said one final goodbye before they began making their way down the road to the main gate.

Runner was waiting for them outside the main gate eating a chair that presumably one of the guards had left. As Jariko was preparing Runner, the messenger that Jariko met at the Semos messenger service arrived back at the city.

"Ah good timing! Here," the man said, out of breath. He handed Jariko a letter and then continued to run into the city. Jariko opened the letter. It was from Rolo.

Dear Jariko, I'm glad you're safe and I can't believe you're in Orkestra. I know how much you've always wanted to go so don't feel rushed to come home. We have decided to stay here since nothing is left in Rybalin. Just send word when you can and tell us about any adventures you get into and let me know when you need more medicine. I'll send some with your next letter.

Jariko smiled. He knew the next letter he sent to old man Rolo was going to have some amazing stories.

Jariko finished strapping the bags to Runner, while Kellarom and Irabella were talking to Merlon. Jariko took one more look at the amazing city he had been staying in and couldn't help but smile.

They all said their goodbye to Merlon and promised they would stay in touch with any information they found, just so he knew they were okay and not getting into too much trouble. Merlon waved them goodbye as they made their way down the long road and just like that, they were off on the greatest adventure of their lives, no idea what they were getting into or the danger that awaited them in the pirate-ruled lands of Tortu.

Printed in Great Britain
by Amazon

87380432R00163